Cherokee Rose

By

Nancy McIntosh Pafford

Edited by Amy Ammons Garza

Illustrated by Doreyl Ammons Cain

Catch the Spirit of Appalachia, Inc.
Western North Carolina

FIRST PRINTING 2006

Note to the Reader: The story of Cherokee Rose and other characters are fictional.

Cover Illustration by Doreyl Ammons Cain

Published by
SAN NO. 8 5 1 – 0 8 8 1
Catch the Spirit of Appalachia, Inc.
29 Regal Avenue, Sylva, NC 28779
Phone: 828-631-4587

Library of Congress Control Number: 2006930092

ISBN-13: 978-0-9753023-5-4
ISBN-10: 0-9753023-5-3

Dedicated to the Cherokee Elders

It is with great respect and admiration that I have dedicated my book ***Cherokee Rose*** to our Cherokee elders. They are today's treasures...sharing their wisdom and passing on Cherokee history, culture and traditions for tomorrow.

Sharing the Cherokee lifestyle with Rose in this book is the character "Grandpa" who is modeled after some of the elders from the Eastern Band of Cherokee Indians on the Qualla Boundary in Cherokee, NC. Below are what a few of them have said when asked what they think is important today.

—Nancy M. Pafford, Author

"Listen to all elders, learn all the wisdom and knowledge you can while they're still here. Don't be afraid to ask."

—Maybelle Sequoyah McDonald

"We should share our customs and traditions with our children."

—David Ned Smith, Sr.

"I feel that education is important to our young people because with it the traditional things will be learned."

—Catherine Blythe Sanders

"Learn the culture and history of our people."

—Lizzie Hull

"The main thing is discipline — and this comes from the home. Something very important for young people is to complete an education. And most importantly...learn our Cherokee language, culture and traditions."

—Jerry Wolfe

CONTENTS

CONTENTS

Thank you

To...

THE AMMONS SISTERS...Amy Ammons Garza, my editor, and Doreyl Ammons Cain, my artist. I am grateful to have had the privilege of working with these incredibly talented ladies. Again, it has been an honor.

ZELLNA T. SHAW...my dear, dear friend, who proofread my manuscript, offered helpful suggestions and encouraged me throughout the writing of this book. Her gift of a beautiful hiking stick (carved by Jay Moore) inspired me to include it in the story. The stick is shown on the cover of this book .

TIM PAFFORD...my son. His continued support, encouragement and interest during the writing of this book has brought joy to my heart.

JERRY WOLFE...respected Cherokee elder and special friend. His wisdom and knowledge of the Cherokee history has been a constant source of help to me. Thanks, Jerry, for patiently answering my many questions concerning the culture and lifestyles of the Cherokee people.

DAVID SMITH... Cherokee gallery and market owner and good friend. His promotion and interest in my books have been exceptional. David has opened his doors to me for many booksignings and it is greatly appreciated.

CHEROKEE FRIENDS...Bo Taylor, Annie Jensen, David, Paul, Donald and others who answered my many questions during interviews while writing this book. I am indebted to them.

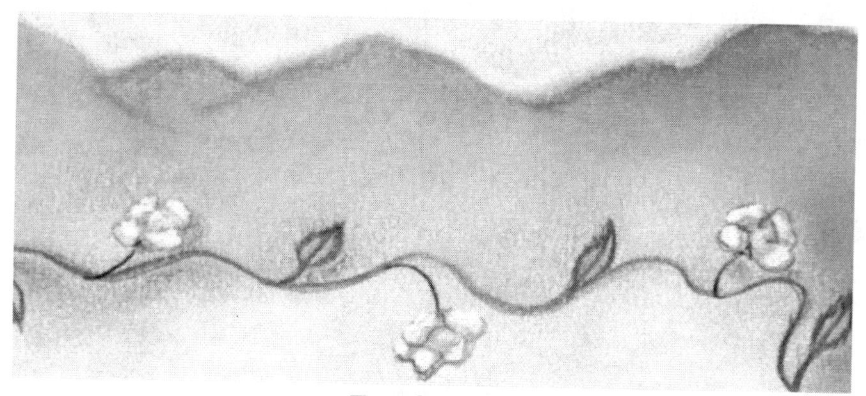

Prologue

The Spirit of White Feather

Spring, 1858—Georgia Homestead

White Feather and Little Fawn sat on the front porch of the frame house facing the river, watching the young couple down by the river. Gv-nv-ge Yo-na (Black Bear) and Gloria held hands, oblivious to others. During their conversation they laughed often.

"Those two are in love, Mother," Little Fawn said, smiling. She moved her infant daughter from her lap to her shoulder and continued rocking the baby.

"Yes, I think you are right," White Feather agreed.

"There will be a wedding soon, don't you think?"

"Perhaps."

"Gloria will be a good wife for my brother."

Her mother nodded. "Yes," she said.

"I'm happy Tsu-la (Red Fox) and his family moved back to the mountains from the western territory."

"That was good...Yes."

White Feather remembered that Tsa-la's family had fallen in love with the mountainous land on their first visit. When they returned the next year for another visit Tsu-la had surprised everyone by announcing that he and his family had come to stay. Almost immediately he had purchased a farm and built a large store next door to Michael's livery stable in the small settlement nearby.

"Mother, there is something that I have never told you."

"And what is that, my daughter?"

"I am happy that you married Michael," Little Fawn began softly. "He has been good to Gv-nv-ge Yo-na and me. And..." she said warmly, looking at her mother, "he has been a good husband to you too, bringing you much happiness."

"Yes, he has," White Feather smiled, nodding her head.

"This big house he built for you by the river is beautiful," Little Fawn said, motioning with her hand. Again White Feather nodded in agreement.

"I love Michael very much but I wish I had more memories of my father. I was so young when he died on 'the trail where they cried.' I can't remember much about him except being carried in his arms on our walk to the western Indian Territory."

Glancing out into the yard Little Fawn continued. "You have told me that my father built the chimney himself. Each time I look at it I think of him."

"I am glad. He chose the rocks from the river and brought them up the hill to build the chimney. He was very of proud of it."

"It's still beautiful," Little Fawn said, glancing at the stone structure, "even after your cabin burned,"

"Yes. It is good it survived."

The chimney held many memories for White Feather and she was glad that it stood close, nearby. One memory that truly delighted her was remembering how her children had enjoyed it during their childhood. They built fires within its fireplace during the cooler days when playing outside and stood before it to warm themselves so they could remain outside and play longer. And it had made her very happy when Little Fawn and her husband, a Cherokee man whose family had hidden in the mountains to escape being captured by the soldiers, had married in the shade of the big chimney two summers ago.

"Your father loved you and Gv-nv-ge Yo-na very much." White Feather smiled at her daughter.

The two women continued to rock quietly, each lost in her own thoughts.

Just as Little Fawn's half brother, Tsa-li (Charlie) and Wade, Tsu-la's son, came into White Feather's mind, Little Fawn spoke. "I'll be glad when Tsa-li and Wade come home. I miss them."

"Yes. It seems as if they have been away at school forever," laughed White Feather, realizing once again how the two of them thought alike.

"And I'm sure that Michael and Tsu-la...and Gv-nv-ge Yo-na will be glad to have the extra help in the store and livery stable.

Little Fawn nodded, slowly rising from her chair.

"The baby is asleep now. I will go in and put her to bed and perhaps take a nap myself," she whispered softly.

"I think I will stay here on the porch for a while longer. Michael will be home soon and I want to be out here to greet my husband when he arrives," White Feather said as her daughter left to go inside the house.

White Feather gazed at the blue-green mountains surrounding her home. Leaning her head back in the chair, she relaxed and closed her eyes. She continued rocking while she thought back to the time eighteen years ago when she came home from the West.

She would never forget the day she had seen the mountains again. She felt that she had been greeted by old, dear friends. She recalled how the birds had called out to her with their joyful songs welcoming her home. She had heard the water cascading over rocks in the river and remembered how the familiar sound had made her heart leap in anticipation of seeing the river again.

A vision of Running Deer, her first husband, the young Cherokee man she loved so deeply, appeared in her mind. She stopped rocking, opened her eyes and turned to look at the tall stone chimney in the yard.

"Running Deer," White Feather whispered, "I will never forget that your gift of the gold nugget provided us a way to come home. Thank you."

Putting her hand over her heart she whispered again. "I will always love you. You will remain in my heart forever."

White Feather's gaze traveled back to the surrounding mountains. She watched while the lowering sun cast its shadows on the mountains, streaking them in shades of green.

White Feather smiled.

"This is my home," she said aloud. "My heart and spirit will always remain here."

"Remembering White Feather, I believe her undying spirit will move forever among the tranquil hills and valleys of her home." (Taken from the author's epilogue in her first book "WHITE FEATHER.")

—Nancy McIntosh Pafford, 2006

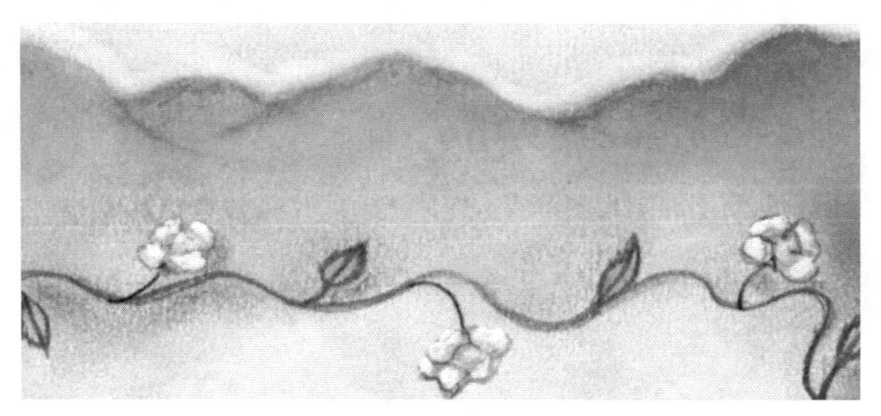

CHAPTER ONE
A Cherokee Rose Bush

Six generations later...

Grandmother, this has been a beautiful trip through the mountains," the young girl said.

"Yes, it has been," answered the woman driving the car, her gaze leaving the road briefly to glance out the window toward the river. "Look how the water sparkles in the sunlight as it winds its way down the mountains." She turned slightly to look at the mountains streaked in shadowy colors on the other side of the road. "And look how the sunshine bathes the mountains in different shades of green," she added, nodding toward the ridges in front of them.

The car turned often as it moved along the

road through the tall mountains, following curves that hugged the meandering river.

"See those flowers growing by the river," Janie said, pointing toward the water. "What kind are they, Grandmother?"

"Those are rhododendron. Their pink blooms are plentiful this time of the year."

"They are so pretty."

"Yes, they are."

Rose and her Granddaughter had left Rose's home two hours earlier, traveling on winding roads through the newness of spring. Now Janie was becoming restless to arrive.

"You have made this trip such a secret, Grandmother. When are you going to tell me where we are going?"

Rose smiled at the twelve-year-old Janie. Such a lovely child, she thought, admiring Janie's dark eyes and raven-colored hair. "You will see before long. We'll be there soon. See...we've just traveled into Georgia," Rose nodded at the roadside sign as they passed it.

"Aren't you even going to give me a hint?"

"Nope!" Rose laughed, glancing at Janie, thinking how pleased she was to have Janie visiting her for the summer. Rose had looked forward to this day for many years. This would be the day Janie would learn of her heritage.

A short time later Rose slowed the car and pulled over to the parking area by the river. "Here we are," she said brightly. "Come on, let's go."

"But, Grandmother, we've already seen the river," Janie said, glancing toward the water.

"Not the river, honey. Come on...get out of the car and come with me."

Janie followed her Grandmother across the road. When they reached the bottom of a small rise Rose motioned for her to follow.

"Come," she said, and they began walking up the hill.

When they reached the top Janie stopped and slowly turned in a circle looking around her, her arms outstretched.

"This is a cemetery, Grandmother," she said, her hand pointing to the graveyard. "Is this what you wanted me to see?" she asked, disappointment in her voice.

"Yes, now follow me. I want you to look at the names on the markers."

They slowly made their way between the graves, stopping to read some of the inscriptions.

"Grandmother, these graves are really old," Janie said, motioning to the head rocks, many broken with age.

"Yes, they are," Rose responded, watching while the young girl moved from grave to grave, pleased that Janie's interest was growing.

"It's hard to read some of the names," Janie said, leaning down closer to the graves. "Wade, Charlie, Gloria, Marie...and Grandmother, look at this unusual name...Little Fawn. Come look!"

Rose smiled, nodding her head.

They continued walking through the cemetery, heads bent low, looking at the writing on each headstone.

"Grandmother! Come here! Look at this one...Tsu-la. I've never heard that name before! There's only one name on the marker...no last name, just like most of the others. Do you know who these people were?"

Without answering Rose continued to follow Janie from grave to grave.

"I can't read this one at all...Gu-nv-ge Yo-na," Janie said, saying the letters in the name. "Who was that?"

"Oh," Rose laughed softly, "that's Gu-nv-ge Yo-na...Black Bear's grave."

Janie turned and looked at Rose in surprise. "How can you read these names? They look strange to me," she said, moving her head from side to side.

"Most of the people buried here are Indian people," Rose said quietly, "Cherokee Indian people. These graves are very, very old. Come, let's move to the center of the cemetery."

Janie followed, the look on her face testifying to the still unanswered question as to why her Grandmother had brought her to see an old cemetery.

When they reached the middle of the burial grounds, Rose stopped and pointed to a grave. "This is the oldest grave here," she said, motioning to the grave in front of her.

Janie stooped down to look closer at the worn rock, cracked and broken in several places.

"I can't make out this name at all. It looks like a V or W something." She stood and shook her head, "Look at all of these big rocks piled up beside the grave."

Rose nodded.

"There's a big weed growing beside the grave. It's covered in thorns! I'll pull it up and throw it away." Janie reached for the plant.

"NO! No! Don't touch it!"

Startled, Janie drew her hand away, stood

and looked at her Grandmother in surprise.

"Why not, Grandmother? It's just a weed."

"No. It is a Cherokee Rose bush. It will have beautiful white blooms on it soon. It was planted here many, many years ago."

Janie looked back at the plant while her Grandmother continued.

"It is a survivor...just like these people were," she said, motioning to the graves around her. "These people survived the Trail of Tears...the removal from their homeland by the army to Oklahoma in 1838. They only returned home when they were allowed to come back."

"How do you know all about this, Grandmother?"

"It's a long story," Rose smiled at Janie.

"Tell me, Grandmother, please, tell me," Janie said, tugging on her Grandmother's sleeve.

"Come, let's sit on the rocks beside the grave," Rose said.

Rose eased herself down on a large rock beside Janie. She straightened her back, put her hands on her knees, sighed, and looked around.

"Listen, Janie. There is a creek nearby. Can you hear the water running?"

Janie nodded, listening intently as she became more aware of her surroundings.

"And look up at the trees waving gently in the breeze...and oh, see!" Rose said, pointing to a lower limb of the tree in front of them. Nestled in the green of the tree sat a bright red bird, who had paused briefly from flight to sing a song for them.

They sat in silence for a moment, listening, not moving.

"Please, Grandmother, I want to hear the story."

With a far away look in her eyes heightened by memory Rose's voice took on a softened tone as she told the story...

"Well...it all began a long, long time ago...when I first arrived in North Carolina from the west and began teaching school."

"You taught school?"

"Yes. I taught second grade at the Indian Reservation School for many years."

"Why did you go there, Grandmother?"

"Well, I didn't know why at the time. I was just drawn there for some reason I didn't understand."

"When did you find out why you moved there?"

"Oh, that came later. It's part of the story I'm about to tell you."

"Didn't you have friends where you lived before? Weren't they unhappy when you moved away? Didn't they want you to stay?"

"Yes," Rose laughed softly. "One, in particular, as I remember."

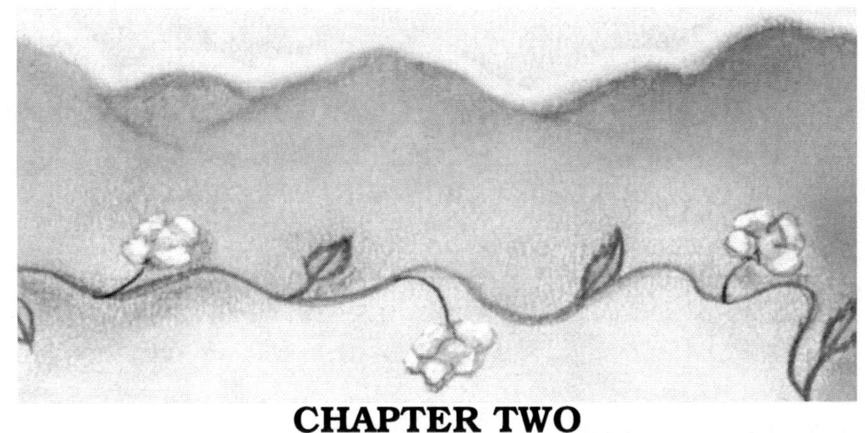

CHAPTER TWO

The Indian Reservation

1956-Summer

"Do you mean to tell me that you want to go traipsing half-way across the country alone to some Indian reservation that you know nothing about?"

"Yes."

"To live?"

"Yes."

"Have you lost your mind?"

Silence.

Rose simply stared at Greg. The disbelief that darkened his face told Rose all she needed to know. The short, stocky man rose, now red-faced, and stomped around the room.

"You can't be serious," his voice rising with each word. "Why, Rose? Why?"

"Please try to understand, Greg. I feel that I must go."

"Must go?" Once again Greg's voice rose.

"Yes, I have to go."

"Rose," Greg stopped pacing and stretched out his hand to touch her arm. "Do you have to go?"

Rose shook her head slowly, "I can't explain the reason."

"You can't explain!" Greg moved away to look out the front window, his back to her.

Greg's agitation and confusion caused by Rose's sudden announcement was apparent in the tension of his body and the tone of his voice. He was struggling to understand and to keep some degree of reason, but it seemed he was coming close to loosing the inner battle he was fighting.

With firm determination in her voice Rose continued, "Well, I only know that I am drawn there for some reason."

Greg sighed, stuffed his hands in his pockets and moved his head from side to side. He was silent for a moment, then turned, crossed the room and sat down beside Rose. Taking her hand he said softly, "Rose, Look at me."

Rose turned to face Greg.

"What about us, Rose? Don't I mean anything to you?"

"Yes, of course. You are my friend, Greg, but..."

"Friend?" he choked. "You don't care enough to stay here and marry me?"

"Marry?" Surprised, Rose pulled her hand away.

"Yes. Won't you stay here and marry me?"

Rose looked down, thoughts racing through her mind. The idea of marrying Greg had never occurred to her. Yes, they had dated during the past year, but marriage had never been discussed. She liked Greg, enjoyed his company, but she didn't love him, at least not in the way that would lead to marriage.

"Rose?"

"No, Greg, I care for you, but I can't marry you," she said quietly. Rose stood and moved to the other side of the room.

Greg shook his head. "Rose, come back. Please sit down," he said, motioning to the sofa.

Rose eased herself onto the opposite end of the sofa away from Greg and stared at her hands clasped tightly in her lap.

"Rose, I will miss you and your friends will miss you. School is out for the summer. We can have fun together...take a trip...or whatever you want to do," he said in a final plea.

"No," she whispered.

Silence.

Still in shock as to what was becoming evident, Greg asked, "When are you leaving?"

"Next week," she answered.

It proved to be a busy week. Greg was not the only one surprised by Rose's plan to move so far from her home to accept a teaching position in an Indian school. Her friends were as confused as Greg and everyone tried to convince her she was making a mistake. However, Rose held firm in her decision. She was eagerly anticipating the challenge and secretly anxious to find the reason for this unexplainable need to begin the new venture in her life. Something inside of her told her that this was the right thing to do.

1956 – Early Fall

Rose sat behind her desk in front of the classroom, her gaze sweeping over her dark-haired second grade students while they completed their class assignment. She had been their teacher for two months, and Rose had grown to love all of "her kids."

She stood, walked to the window and glanced toward the cumulus cloud formations in the sky. She stared at them for a moment and then at the ridges of blue-green mountains in the distance. Their beauty had come to warm her heart each time she looked at them.

I am home, she thought. This is where I am supposed to be...here in the land of the Cherokee.

She turned quickly when she heard a small voice near the back of the room call out.

"Miss Rose, it's time to go home."

"Yes," she said, smiling at her students, "yes, it is."

She glanced back and looked at the mountains again. "I have come home," she whispered. "I feel it in my heart."

"Grandmother, you have always been happy here, haven't you?" Janie asked.

"Oh yes," Rose smiled.

"What happened next, Grandmother?" Janie said, leaning her elbows on Rose's knees and looking into her face, anxiously waiting for her Grandmother to continue the story.

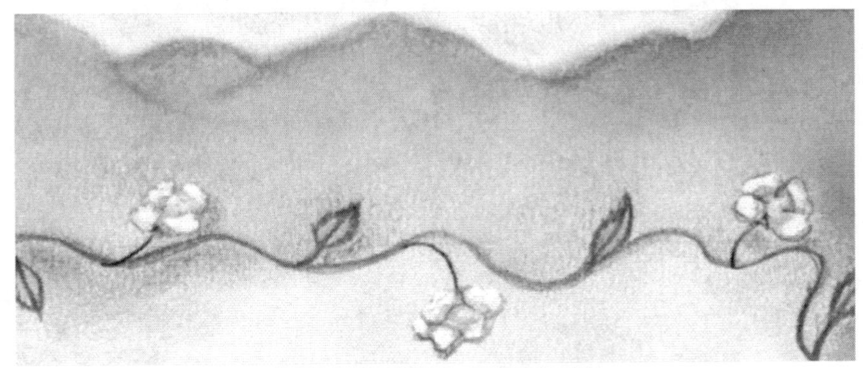

CHAPTER THREE

The Invitation

The Grandmother's story continued....

Several weeks later the young Rose stood near the window watching the yellow buses loaded with noisy children leave the school. Slowly her gaze moved toward the mountains. The early colors of fall were making their way down the mountainsides.

Soon they will all be in blazing colors of autumn, she thought, as she walked to her desk to begin gathering things to take home. She looked forward to a restful weekend, spending time in her front porch swing reading a new book.

Turning to leave her classroom she was startled by a muffled knock on the door.

The door creaked. Dovey, one of her students, and her father stood looking into the room.

"May we come in?" the man said.

"Yes, of course, please come in," Rose replied.

She had, in the past, noted and admired the interest he had shown for Dovie.

"Miss Rose...."

"Please, just call me Rose," she interrupted, smiling and thinking that they had come to possibly discuss Dovie's schoolwork. She sat down at her desk.

"All right...Rose...people call me...uh, Hunter," he said, not sitting. "I've come to ask you something."

"Yes?"

"Dovie has been pestering me for weeks to take her on a picnic before the days become too cold to go."

"Yes, I know," Rose laughed. "She mentions it almost every day."

"Well, since the warm days will not last much longer we plan to go tomorrow."

"Oh, that's good. It will make Dovie very happy."

"We want you to come with us."

The invitation surprised Rose and for a moment she did not respond.

"That's nice of you, but...."

"Please say you will go."

"I don't know. I have to...."

"Please don't say no. Dovie will be so disappointed if you do not go," he said, then added, "and I will be also. We haven't gone on a picnic since her mother...passed."

Rose still hesitated, but thinking that it would be a nice outing, she began to consider going with them. "I don't know…maybe."

Hunter seized the moment. "Dovie is taking one of her little friends and we really want you to come too. Say yes, please," Hunter insisted, smiling.

"Well, I suppose I could, but…."

"Good!" Hunter grinned. "We'll pick you up at 11:00." He quickly grabbed the hand of the smiling Dovie, who had been hiding behind him, and told her in a loud whisper, "Let's get out of here before she changes her mind."

Hunter walked rapidly toward the door almost as if he was afraid that Rose would decide not to go with them. "See you in the morning," he said, going out the door.

Rose could hear Dovie's giggle as they scurried out of sight. She smiled.

Almost immediately Hunter appeared once again in the doorway. "I'll bring the food." And then he was gone.

She left her classroom feeling light-hearted and anticipating the picnic. Her thoughts focused on Dovie's father…he was very handsome. She really knew nothing about the man except that he was a polite, concerned single parent who apparently loved his beautiful little daughter.

Rose shook her head and smiled. A picnic will be nice, I suppose, she thought. This warm weather won't last much longer and the leaves on the trees are so beautiful…perhaps she and Dovie's father would become friends. She shook her head and smiled.

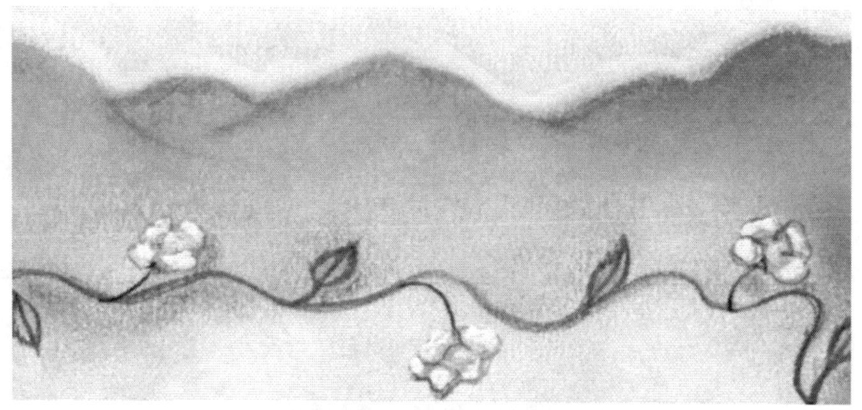

CHAPTER FOUR
The Picnic

Dovie's father had driven to a beautiful park for the picnic. They had walked across a bridge to arrive at the picnic area. The park had tall trees with colorful leaves dipping down into a shallow river. Water surrounded the picnic area and Rose felt like they were on an island. Tiny wild flowers grew along the banks of the water in a variety of colors that blended with the vibrant dark greens that would soon turn to reds, bronze and golds. Birds sang their songs in the trees and lively squirrels were scampering in every direction hiding acorns and other nuts for the cold winter months ahead. Rose marveled at the beauty around her.

Soon they spread out the meal on a heavy green blanket, laughing and watching the children play when they finished eating.

It was a good day, pleasant and easy, a lazy farewell to the busy days of autumn, but an eager welcome to the slower time of winter.

As the day drew to a close, Rose began packing up the remainder of the food in the picnic basket. She hated to have the day end. She had enjoyed the companionship and the instant camaraderie she and Hunter had shared.

Dovie ran up. "Daddy, can we wade in the river?" she asked, as she pulled her friend to her side.

"It's very cold," Hunter laughed.

"Please! Please! We don't care!"

"All right, but stay where I can see you and...."

"Thank you!" cried both girls while they once again ran toward the water.

"...and be careful on the rocks," Hunter finished, raising his voice.

Hunter stretched his arms over his head, criss-crossed them behind his neck, and then lay down on his back across the blanket. He watched Rose, thinking how beautiful she looked. The pink blouse and slacks she wore complimented her dark skin and hair.

"The food was delicious," she said, closing the basket. She sat down beside him and added, "Please tell your mother how much I enjoyed it." Then quickly guessed, "She did pack the lunch, didn't she?"

"Yes...I will...and she did," Hunter answered, raising himself to a sitting position, never taking his eyes off the young woman. "Tell me about yourself, Rose."

"Oh, there's really not much to tell. I was born in Oklahoma, an only child. My parents died in a car accident when I was young."

"I'm sorry."

"Thank you," said Rose. Pausing for a moment she continued, "I have no memory of them and know nothing about them."

"Nothing?"

"No," she said, shaking her head. "Through the years I asked family members to tell me about them and they would say that they didn't know anything. I always thought that it was strange because I felt they should have known something. It was like they didn't want to tell me."

Hunter shook his head as Rose continued.

"I was passed among family members until my Grandmother took me into her home and raised me. She sent me to college," Rose paused, then continued, "and passed away right after I graduated. She left the house to me so I lived in it until I sold it...and now here I am!" She smiled, the look on her face made Hunter think she may have told him too much.

"It's sad that you do not know your family."

"Like I said...here I am, and very happy, I must add," she laughed.

"I am glad," Hunter said softly, looking into Rose's dark eyes, realizing for the first time in five years that he had been drawn to a woman. Surprised, he could feel the desire to take her into his arms. I like her smile, he thought, and the way her eyes twinkle. Pulled in by them, he knew that he had literally been caught...all she had to do was reel him in. At the thought, he laughed softly.

Their eyes held for a few moments before the spell was broken but not before Rose thought she heard a soft whisper but couldn't make out the words. She shook herself slightly and looked at Hunter.

"I like Dovie's name," Rose said, obviously attempting to change the subject.

"It's a nickname. We began calling her Dovie when she was a baby because her infant cooing sounded so much like a dove. Her Cherokee name is Ah-yo-ka. It means 'she who brought happiness.' It was the name of the daughter of Sequoyah, the great Cherokee who invented our written language."

Rose nodded. "And you, Hunter, tell me about yourself. How did you get the name Hunter?"

"It's a nickname too," he laughed. "I've always liked to hunt and be alone in the woods. When I wanted to be by myself as a youngster I would take my gun and go into the forest and spend the night."

"Do you still like to hunt?"

"Oh, yes!"

"What else?"

"I met my wife when I was in college in New Mexico. After we married we both taught school. Dovie was born when we had been married two years. When my wife died...Dovie was three...we came back home. Mother wanted us to live with her and Grandpa so she could help with Dovie. That's where we've been for the past five years."

"Are you teaching now?"

"No, I write books and have made a living selling them and I also...."

"Daddy! Daddy!" Dovie interrupted, running toward Hunter, "Look what I found!" She fell into Hunter's lap and extended her hand toward him. "Look at the pretty rock I found in the river!"

` Hunter took the stone and turned it over in his hand.

"It's beautiful, Dovie. You have found a treasure."

"Keep it for me," she said, jumping up and running toward the river.

Hunter smiled at Rose, thinking that he, too, had found a treasure today...the first one in a long, long time and he wanted to keep it also.

After Rose returned home from the picnic she immediately went to the telephone and called Tara, the school nurse, who had befriended her.

Tara had become Rose's closest friend since moving to the east and began teaching school. The two young women of the same age had liked each other from their first meeting when school began.

Rose had mentioned to some of the teachers in the school lounge that she was living in the local motel and looking for a place to live. Tara had entered the room, sat down, and was listening to Rose.

She spoke up immediately. "You must see Aunt Vi's rooming house. It's a big beautiful old home and several of our teachers live there. I know that she still has an apartment for rent. Are you interested?"

"Yes!" Rose responded immediately

"If you aren't busy after school, I'll take you over to her house."

"I'd love to go."

"You'll like Aunt Vi. She really isn't my aunt...she belongs to the whole community and everyone calls her their aunt," Tara said. "She has no family of her own here and spends most of her time in the small shop beside her home where she sews Native American clothing and cooks scrumptious food for her adopted families. You'll like her."

After school the two young women went to see Aunt Vi. Rose rented the apartment as soon as she saw it and Aunt Vi became her "aunt" also.

Early that next Saturday morning Tara arrived at the motel. "Come on," she said, picking up a suitcase. "Get a move on. We're going to get you moved to Aunt Vi's."

Rose welcomed the help and soon she was settled in her new home.

Tara, a Cherokee who had lived on the reservation all her life, was a pretty young woman with dark eyes that crinkled when she laughed. She wore her long black hair down around her shoulders most of the time, but she occasionally worked it into braids. She had been very helpful to Rose, not only in finding her a place to live but also at school and in the community, taking her on a tour of the area and introducing her to many of the local people.

Since Tara was alone herself, she and Rose spent a great deal of time together, even taking a few overnight trips to surrounding areas. From the beginning Rose had been drawn in by her new friend's quick smile and as time went on she grew to love the Cherokee woman's sense of humor and contagious laugh.

"Tara, are you busy?" Rose asked when her friend answered the telephone

"No, and it's Saturday night," she moaned and then laughed. "Did you go with Hunter on the picnic?"

"Yes," she answered, pausing for a moment. "Tara, can you come over? I really need to talk to you."

"You sound serious."

"I am."

"I'll be right over."

"Thank you. I'll make coffee."

A short time later when Tara arrived they kicked off their shoes and settled themselves on the sofa with cups of coffee in their hands.

"Go ahead, Rose. What gives?" Tara asked between sips.

"I need to talk to you about two things," Rose began seriously.

"Two things?" Tara leaned closer to Rose, her interest growing.

"Yes."

"Well, please, go ahead. I'm dying of curiosity."

"I spent the afternoon with Hunter and two girls," Rose began.

"Yes?"

"He kissed me!" Rose blurted out, raising her voice.

"What?" Tara smiled.

"He kissed me…Hunter kissed me!"

Tara smiled again.

"It happened so fast. When he brought me

home and started to leave...he kissed me on the cheek," Rose said, placing her hand on her cheek.

"Oh, for heaven's sakes, Rose." Tara started laughing.

"Tara, I'm supposed to have a boyfriend already," Rose said.

"Rose, you hardly ever hear from Greg any-more."

"But I know he is planning to come for Thanksgiving," she said softly, looking down at her coffee cup.

Tara did not respond.

The two women sat quietly for a moment, and then Tara put her hand on Rose's arm and spoke. "Okay. That's one thing you wanted to talk about. What's the other?"

"When Hunter kissed me," Rose said, looking up at Tara, "I liked it."

"What woman wouldn't?" Tara laughed. "He's gorgeous!"

"But it's too fast...too early."

"Follow your heart, Rose," Tara said. "Hunter is a fine, decent man."

"I'm sure he is. I'm just making too much out of it, I suppose."

"Listen, I'm sorry to leave you, but I really have to run," Tara said over her shoulder as she took her cup to the kitchen.

"Do you have to leave so soon?"

"Yes. I'll call you tomorrow," she said, returning to the room. She hugged Rose, and then looked into her eyes. "If he kissed you on the cheek, Rose, I bet he cares for you."

"Do you really think so?"

Tara hugged Rose again, stepped back and

smiled. "You'll see. When he does it again, just listen to the whispers of your heart."

Rose shivered. She watched Tara close the door and as she strolled to the kitchen she wondered...does your heart whisper?

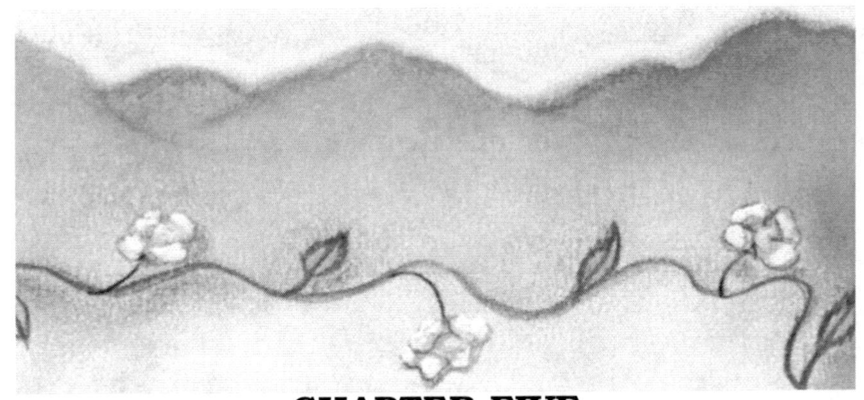

CHAPTER FIVE

Rejected

Autumn leaves covered the mountainsides with brilliant colors. Rose couldn't resist taking long rides to enjoy them. She explored back roads where she had not gone before and she marveled at the vibrant foliage on the trees.

Hunter was never far from her thoughts.

Rose had enjoyed the picnic with Hunter, but it had been unsettling also. She had surprised herself by responding to his kiss and could not erase it from her mind. She actually felt guilty about it. Greg was coming to visit soon, in two weeks, so she decided that she wouldn't think about Hunter anymore...except it was hard to do with Dovie in her classroom each day. She continued to see Hunter at school when he came to pick up Dovie or attend parent meetings. He never mentioned the picnic, and Rose could not understand his actions or aloofness when she saw him. She supposed that the kiss did not mean anything to him...or perhaps he was busy writing. He had told her that his new book was nearing completion.

"Oh, I am just being silly about the entire thing," she scolded herself, "what's a little kiss on the cheek?" She still could not get Hunter out of her mind.

She had spoken to Greg on the telephone during the first week after arriving, now seldom heard from him. She didn't mind. Greg was a nice person, but she was not in love with him. Rose had a new life now...however, she did wonder how she would feel when he came to see her during the holidays.

A few days before Thanksgiving Rose's telephone rang very late one evening as she was getting ready for bed.

"Hello."

"Rose?"

"Yes. Oh, Greg! How are you?" she asked, recognizing his voice.

Without answering her question Greg immediately began the purpose of his call.

"Rose, there's something I must tell you," he said solemnly.

"Is something wrong?"

"Well...." Greg's voice faltered.

"What is it?"

"Rose, I'm not coming to visit you at Thanksgiving."

Surprised, Rose could not respond.

"I don't know how to begin, Rose."

She still couldn't say anything.

"You know that I care for you...and I would not want to hurt you."

Rose finally found her voice. She sat down on the bed, aware of the awkwardness in his voice. "Greg, what is it?"

"I missed you after you left."

"Greg, I...."

"Please let me finish, Rose."

"Go on."

"This is hard, Rose," Greg hesitated, then rushed on. "I met someone and we have been dating since you left."

"Oh?"

"We are planning to be married on Christmas Day," Greg blurted out, rushing through the words.

"What!"

"We are getting married."

Everything was quiet.

Rose could hear the ticking of the clock on her night table.

"Rose?"

"I wish you happiness, Greg," she said, and then slowly hung up the phone.

Stunned at the sudden news, Rose felt the rejection. Surprisingly then, relief took over. She had been invited out on dates several times but would not go because of Greg. Now she would feel free to go out and meet some of the young people in town and have fun. And she could think about Hunter.

She was glad that Greg had found someone. Never was she going back to her former home.

She knew that now. Her life was here, in a place where she now felt she belonged. Her heart pounded! Now she could put complete closure on her former life and think about Hunter.

Rose awakened Thanksgiving morning with mixed emotions. In the few days since Greg had called with his surprising news Rose had had time to reflect on her past and wonder about her future. She realized she wanted to know more about herself and the reason she had been compelled to come to the reservation to live.

But for today Rose decided she would just relax and enjoy her new life—a life that was now only hers to shape as she chose.

Suddenly she realized she was hungry and had not prepared a Thanksgiving meal. She grabbed her jacket off the coat rack in her living room and walked toward town, hoping she could find a restaurant that would be open on the holiday. Just as she passed Aunt Vi's little store she heard her voice.

"Happy Thanksgiving, Rose."

Rose turned to see Aunt Vi standing in the doorway of her little shop, waving her hand.

"Where's your friend? I'd like to meet him," she called.

"He's not coming, Aunt Vi."

"Oh, I'm sorry."

Rose really did not want to discuss Greg with Aunt Vi, but she also didn't want to be rude to this kind lady. She shrugged and said, "He had an unexpected turn of events and wasn't able to make the trip."

"So you'll be having dinner alone?"

"Yes, Aunt Vi. I suppose I will."

With much pleasure and a gleam in her eyes Aunt Vi came to Rose and put her arm around her. "No, girl, you won't...come on in here."

Rose didn't hesitate. The two women walked arm-in-arm up the steps. The cozy shop was filled with a wonderful aroma of coffee and home-made cinnamon buns cooling on the counter.

Aunt Vi chattered away while Rose listened and ate the plateful of food her new friend had prepared. She was glad that Greg's name did not come up again.

"And my family's in Pennsylvania so I don't get to see them often, but I'm going up there for Christmas this year," Aunt Vi was saying just as Rose finished eating one of the buns.

"I'm glad you will see them, Aunt Vi...and I'm sure that they will be glad to see you too."

"Yes. We have a good time together."

By the time Rose left for her own home the two women had become fast friends and were destined to share many hours together in the future.

As Rose walked along she listened contentedly to the soft sounds of winter drifting all about her. She surveyed the mountains and the crisp sky above and smiled. Never had she been happier.

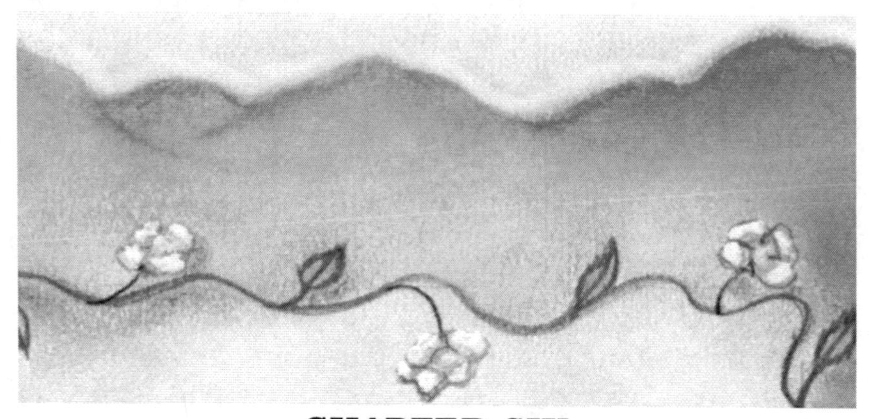

CHAPTER SIX

Not Alone for Christmas

Christmas was fast approaching and the children in Rose's class had been bursting with excitement in anticipation of the coming holidays. Tomorrow would be the last day of school before their Christmas vacation. Now school was out for the day and all the students had left the room except Dovie.

"Aren't you riding the bus today, Dovie?"

"No. Daddy's coming to get me and he wants to talk to you."

"Oh?"

"Yes," Dovie said, giggling.

Just as Rose sat down at her desk there was a soft knock on the door and Hunter eased it open.

"Can I come in?" he asked softly.

"Yes, of course," Rose smiled, glad to see Hunter, and motioned for him to enter.

Dovie ran into her Daddy's arms, hugging him, and then whispering in his ear.

"Yes, I am, Dovie."

He turned to Rose. "Rose, we want to ask you a question."

Dovie smiled.

"All right."

"Do you have plans for Christmas Day?"

"Well, no, not really," she answered, secretly thinking that the day was going to be lonely for her with no family or friends around.

"We know that you have friends here, but we want to be the first to ask you to join us for Christmas dinner."

The invitation surprised Rose. "That's very nice of you, but...."

"Please, Miss Rose," begged Dovie.

"There will only be Mother, Grandpa...certainly Dovie and me...and you, if you will come."

"Please," Dovie begged.

"Yes. Please say yes," added Hunter. "We want you to be a part of our family Christmas."

"I wouldn't want to be any trouble."

"Not at all. Mother and Grandpa are anxious to meet you."

"Well, all right, if you are sure that I won't be intruding."

"Great!" It was clear that Hunter was very pleased by her acceptance.

Dovie jumped up and down, squealing and clapping her hands.

"What can I bring?"

"Only yourself. Dovie and I will pick you up

at two o'clock on Christmas Day."

"Thank you. I look forward to going."

Rose smiled as she watched Hunter and Dovie leave the room, hand in hand.

"Christmas," the word eased from Rose's lips like satin. "I won't be alone like all those years of the past," she whispered softly.

Rose stood and went to the window and looked up at the puffy white clouds and in them she saw a vision of Christmas of long ago. A little girl stood alone and watched while a family sat around a Christmas tree, opening gifts, laughing and talking among themselves, ignoring the child no one wanted.

Rose recognized herself...and all the Christmases of her childhood. She was the little girl moved from one home to another, tolerated only because she had no parents. Rose thought of the invitation she had just received and she smiled. It made her heart happy that she would be with a family this Christmas—a family who seemed to really want her.

Rose could hardly wait for Christmas to arrive.

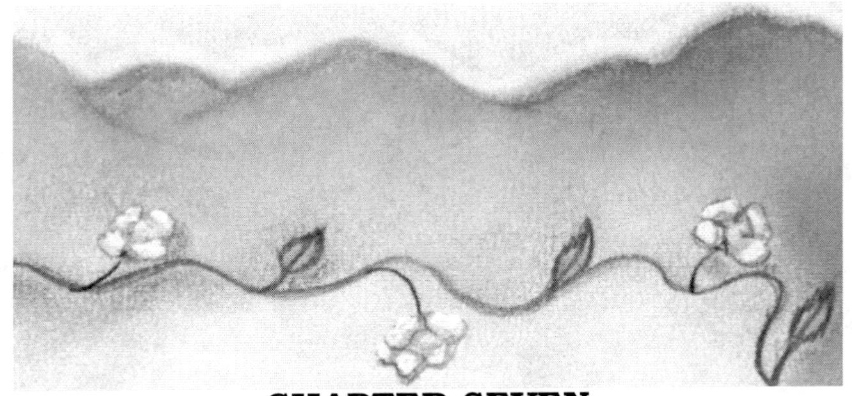

CHAPTER SEVEN

Grandpa

A light snow had fallen on Christmas Eve, adorning the trees and mountainsides. Rose had stood at the window in her home several times off and on looking out at its quiet beauty.

The road to Hunter's home twisted around the mountains and at every turn Rose caught her breath, enjoying the winter scenery of the snowy mountains.

Hunter slowed the truck and turned into a little valley. "This is it," he said.

A large log cabin with smoke rising from the stone chimney sat between two tall fir trees. Beyond the house a mountain stream moved effortlessly around large stone boulders, water rushing over smaller rocks. Snow covered the foliage on the banks of the stream.

"Oh, it's so lovely," Rose exclaimed.

Dovie bounced out of the truck as soon as it stopped. "We're here, Miss Rose!"

Rose stepped out of the truck and slowly turned in a circle, looking at the scenery around her. "It's so beautiful!" she said again while Hunter stood nearby, smiling.

"I'm so glad you're here, Miss Rose," Dovie said, looking at her teacher. "Come on," she said taking Rose's hand. "Let's run to the house."

Hunter smiled again as he watched his daughter and Rose hurry toward the cabin.

The front door swung open before they reached the house. A woman stood in the doorway ready to welcome Rose.

"Come in! Come in!" said Hunter's mother. "This must be Rose, the lady I have heard so much about!"

"Yes, this is Rose," Hunter said as he caught up to them.

"Merry Christmas! Merry Christmas! We are so glad you came."

"Merry Christmas," said Rose. "Thank you for inviting me."

"We're glad to have you," she said, closing the door. "Call me Anna. Here, let me take your coat. Go over to the fire and warm yourself. It's cold today."

Hunter took Rose's arm and led her over to the fireplace, with Dovie trailing closely behind.

"I'm so glad you came, Miss Rose," Dovie said once more, taking her hand.

"Thank you, Dovie. Oh...I love this fireplace," Rose said, looking at the massive rock structure that reached to the ceiling of the room.

"Daddy brought all these rocks from the river," Dovie said, motioning to the fireplace.

"It's truly a sight," said Rose, admiring the native stones, sweeping her hand across one of the large rocks.

Her gaze moved to the mantle. It held Native American pottery, baskets and carvings...below them hung four colorful Christmas stockings. "Beautiful," she said softly.

"The Christmas tree is so-o-o lovely," Rose continued, moving closer to the tall tree in the corner of the room. "Oh, it's a live tree," she added, her hand caressing one of the branches. She leaned closer and sniffed. "It smells wonderful."

'"Daddy cut it down and brought it to us from the woods," Dovie said. "It's a Fraser Fir tree."

"Well, it certainly is beautiful and I love all the pretty decorations." Rose turned and looked at Hunter standing nearby, observing the scene.

"We're all so glad that you are here with us today," he said, not realizing how much Rose appreciated his words.

"Hunter, will you please help Grandpa? He's still in his bedroom," Anna said, placing her hand on Hunter's shoulder. "He's very anxious to meet Rose."

"Certainly."

"Make yourself at home, Rose. I'll just go finish up in the kitchen," Anna said.

"Can I help?"

"No, thank you. Everything's almost ready," Anna called, leaving the room.

"Rose, this is my Grandpa, E-do-ha A-woha-li, Walking Eagle," Hunter said, returning, pushing a wheelchair close to the fireplace. "He's been looking forward to meeting you."

Rose turned and faced Hunter's Grandpa.

He sat straight in his wheelchair and smiled at Rose. His eyes, narrowing when he smiled, looked like dark pools of liquid. His shoulder-length hair was silver-white and was held in place with a yellow and red band around his forehead. Wide shoulders told Rose that he had once been a large man and tall...perhaps as tall as Hunter.

Rose walked to the old Cherokee and extended her hand. "Hello."

"Shi-yo (hello)," the elder greeted Rose in the Cherokee language, observing her closely before taking her hand.

Shaking his hand Rose looked at the ring he wore...a silver band centered with a large turquoise stone. Then releasing his hand she stood in front of him. "I like your shirt, Mr. Eagle," Rose said, noticing the colorful shirt he wore, its colors and ribbons matching his head-band.

"It is a traditional ribbon shirt worn by Cherokee men on special occasions," he said.

"It's colorful."

"Goes well with my jeans and moccasins," he chuckled.

"Grandpa has a very special day coming soon. He's going to celebrate his one hundredth birthday."

"That's wonderful, Mr. Eagle," Rose said respectfully, looking into the dark face, covered with deep wrinkles etched there by time.

The old man smiled. "Call me Grandpa."

"All right...Grandpa."

"Did you see my bear claw?" he asked, motioning to the leather strip around his neck, and pointing to the dark claw hanging from it.

Rose leaned in close and took the claw in her hand. "It's really old, isn't it?" she said and looked directly up into his eyes.

The sides of his eyes wrinkled as his voice dropped so only she could hear.

"This holds the honor of my youth."

"Your youth?"

"Yes. One day we will speak of it again."

The dark claw had grown warm to Rose's touch. She released it, stepped back and shivered.

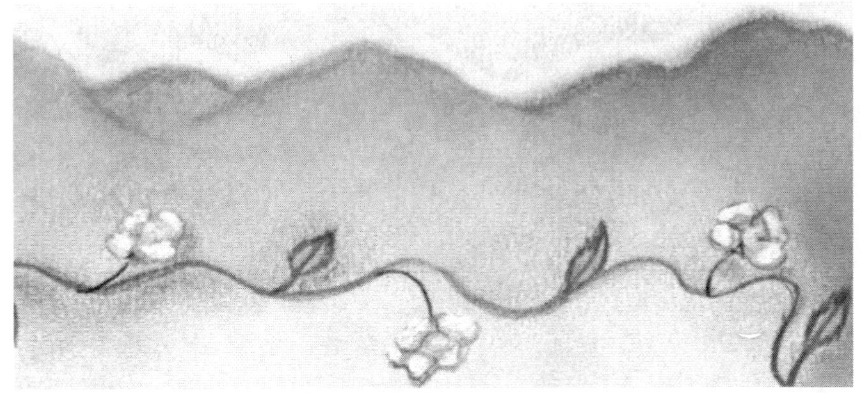

CHAPTER EIGHT

Lone Wolfe

"These paintings are outstanding," Rose said, motioning to the artwork displayed on the living room walls.

She had glanced at the paintings during the meal and was very interested in looking closer at them. Now with the meal over she strolled around the room admiring each one.

"The watercolors are some of the most striking pictures I have ever seen." Leaning closer to one of them, she turned to Hunter. "Were all of these Native American scenes painted by the same person?"

"Yes."

"Whose work is this?" she asked more to herself than Hunter, leaning closer to read the artist's signature at the bottom of the painting.

"Mine."

"No. I mean who is the artist?" she said, thinking that Hunter had misunderstood.

"Lone Wolfe."

"Oh, yes, now I see," she said, pointing to the artist's signature. She turned to Hunter. "I'm reading a book and the author's name is Lone Wolfe. I wonder if it's the same person."

"Yes."

"Who is Lone Wolfe?"

Hunter looked amused. "Me," he answered.

"Hunter, stop teasing me...who is Lone Wolfe?" she asked again.

"Me...I tried to tell you at the picnic that I am an artist but Dovie interrupted to show me her rock."

"What?" Rose turned and looked at Hunter.

"That was what I was trying to tell you."

"You really have talent," she said, turning to look at the artwork again. "When did you paint all of these pictures?"

"Through the years...I've always liked to draw and paint. I started when I was of a young age."

"I've seen your work everywhere on the reservation, but I didn't know that you and Lone Wolfe are the same person," Rose said, admiring Hunter's talents. "So you write...and paint. What talent!"

Hunter smiled.

They moved from painting to painting. At the last one Hunter took Rose by the shoulders and turned her to face him. "I would like it if you called me Lone Wolfe. My family and close friends call me by that name," he said.

"It will take me some time to change from thinking about you as 'Hunter'."

"You think about me, Rose?" His eyes twinkled as he touched her hand.

Rose blushed.

"Did I hear someone mention Lone Wolfe?" Grandpa called from across the room where he had been watching Rose and Hunter.

"Yes. We were discussing my artwork."

"It is good work," Grandpa said, nodding his head.

"Yes, it is," agreed Rose, recovering slightly.

Grandpa's gaze followed Rose while she once again walked from picture to picture.

"Rose, come closer. I want to ask you a question," Grandpa said, motioning for her to come nearer.

She turned and walked to the Cherokee elder and stood before him.

"Rose, how much Cherokee blood do you have in you?"

"Me?"

"Yes."

"What makes you think I have Cherokee blood in me?" Rose questioned.

"I can look at you and tell."

Lone Wolfe walked to Rose's side and lowered his voice, "Grandpa is old, but his mind and insights are sharp. He knows much about our Cherokee people and our history. He is very wise...and he sees beyond the surface."

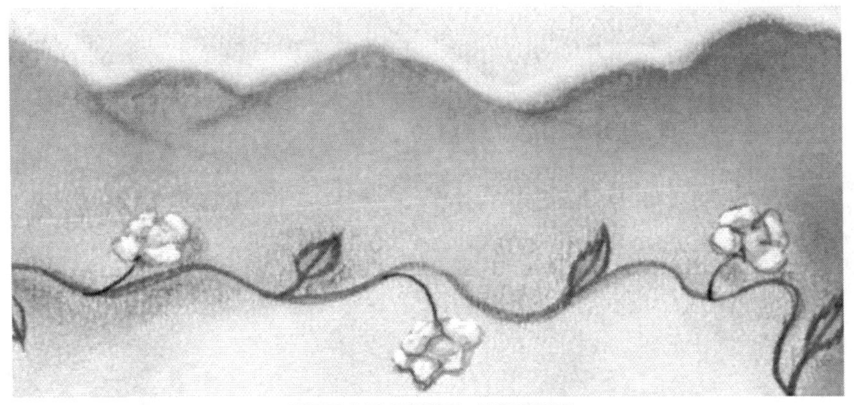

CHAPTER NINE

The Strange Feeling

Several days after Christmas Rose's telephone rang very early in the morning as she was finishing her breakfast.

"Hello."

"Good morning," Lone Wolfe said cheerfully.

"Good morning. How are you today?"

"Fine. Would you like to take a little trip tomorrow?"

"Maybe. Where would we go?"

"Somewhere that Grandpa and I think you will find interesting. We will be gone almost all day."

"All right," Rose said, her interest growing.

"Wear walking shoes."

"Walking shoes?"

"Yes...and a heavy coat."

"Are you going to tell me where we're going?"

"Nope! You'll see soon enough," he laughed. "I'll be at your house early in the morning."

When Rose hung up the phone she wondered why Lone Wolfe would not tell her their destination. But she looked forward to being with him again.

When Lone Wolfe arrived the next morning, they had coffee together before they left. Again she asked him about their trip, but he told her nothing.

Still warm from the coffee Rose went out the door without her jacket, only to hurry back. "I better bundle up," she laughed, pulling on her coat.

With the pickup truck bouncing along a back road, they began their trip through an area that Rose had not seen before. The highway, in need of repair, crossed a beautiful lake and then entered a gorge. A river ran alongside the road with rounded moss-covered rock formations shaping its flow. On the other side of the road tall snow-covered trees adorned the mountains glistening in the sun. The road narrowed and leveled as they went through several small towns before the terrain became hilly again. Finally, Rose saw a sign that said, "Welcome to Georgia."

After stopping for a quick lunch they started on their journey once again.

"We will be there soon, Rose," Lone Wolfe assured her, noticing that she seemed restless.

"I hope so," Rose smiled. Her curiosity was growing rapidly and she was anxious to arrive at the place Lone Wolfe was keeping a secret from her.

They traveled on and shortly the road was sandwiched between a river and tall mountains. After turning a sharp curve Lone Wolfe slowed the truck and parked by the water. He got out and came to Rose's side and opened the door for her.

"Come, Rose, we are here. There is something I want you to see."

Rose pulled on her gloves and gathered her coat tightly in front of her and got out, looking all around. She saw nothing unusual.

Lone Wolfe took her hand, led her across the highway and up a small hill. Their last steps brought them to the top of a rise.

"Here we are. This is what I wanted you to see."

Rose stopped and looked around. "This is a small cemetery," she said, looking at Lone Wolfe in surprise.

"Yes. There are some graves in particular that I would like to show you."

This is strange...why would he want me to see burial grounds, she wondered.

"This is a very old cemetery. Some of my ancestors are buried here, buried long ago after they returned from the West. Have you ever heard of the Trail of Tears?"

"Yes. I know about it," she replied solemnly.

"Come. Look at this grave. This was Grandpa's great, great grandpa," Lone Wolfe said, pointing to an old worn marker. "He has other family and friends buried here too."

They walked slowly around the cemetery. When Rose passed by a grave shadowed by a pile of rocks, a strange feeling shot through her and she shuddered.

A slight breeze had come up and made an eerie sound in the trees and through the hills. It was almost as if the spirits of the past were speaking to them.

Lone Wolfe noticed, took her hand and pulled her close to him. "Are you warm enough? The sun is beginning to be hidden by those dark clouds," he said, motioning to the sky.

Rose did not reply, her eyes on the rocks.

"Are you ready to go back to the truck now?"

"Yes."

Walking back down the hill Rose glanced over her shoulder at the rock formation.

"You know, Lone Wolfe, I feel like I have been to this place before."

"Perhaps in another life," he teased, pulling her close.

They sat silently for a moment when they returned to the truck. Lone Wolfe helped to remove Rose's coat, and moved closer to her side. He traced his fingers up and down her arm, lifted her hand and gently kissed the back of it. Then he turned Rose to face him, gathered her close and kissed her.

"Lone Wolfe...." Rose began to pull away and then suddenly responded.

The trembling man drew her even closer, leaving Rose breathless.

"Lone Wolfe...." Rose shivered.

"You are getting cold, aren't you?"

"Yes," she answered, knowing that it was not the cool air from the river but the effect his kiss had on her. What was this man doing to her? What was it Tara had said to her about listening to the whispers of her heart?

Lone Wolfe ajusted her coat around her shoulders.

"Are you warmer now?" he asked, turning away and starting the vehicle.

Rose nodded.

"It is the cool evening air. I should get you home."

"Thank you for bringing me here today, Lone Wolfe."

As the truck pulled away, an eerie feeling crept up Rose's spine, causing her to glance over her shoulder.

There is something mysterious and magnetic about this place she thought. Then moving closer to Lone Wolfe, she completely forgot everything except the warmth of a budding, deeper mystery.

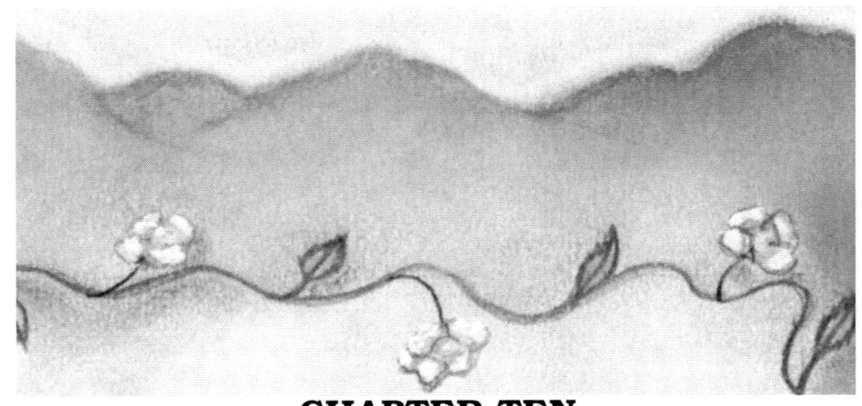

CHAPTER TEN

Quite a Catch

On the trip home Rose filled her heart with the day and continued to feel the warmth of Lone Wolfe's embrace.

The telephone rang while she stood at the door and watched Lone Wolfe drive away.

"What are you doing?" Tara asked when Rose answered the phone.

"Just got in. Why don't you come over?"

"All right. I haven't seen much of you during the holidays."

"I know."

"I made cookies. I'll bring them."

"Good!" laughed Rose. "I need girl talk."

A short time later Tara arrived and the two friends curled up in Rose's living room before a blazing fire, enjoying the cookies and hot chocolate.

"Where have you been? I've called you off and on all day."

"I spent the day with Lone Wolfe."

"Lone Wolfe?" Tara smiled and then took a bite of cookie.

"Yes. Hunter wants me to call him by that name now. We took a trip."

Tara nodded. "All right, go on...go on," said the ever-curious Tara.

"He wouldn't tell me where we were going...only that he and Grandpa wanted me to see a place in north Georgia. We ended up at a beautiful spot by the river and went to a cemetery on top of a hill. Cherokee people are buried there. Have you ever heard of it?"

"Yes."

"You have?"

Tara nodded.

"I can't get the place out of my mind," Rose said. "Now, don't laugh, but the entire time we were in the cemetery I felt like I had been there before."

"Had you?"

"No! How could I have been there?" Rose paused. "It felt strange. It just seemed familiar to me."

"Did you tell Lone Wolfe how you felt?"

"Yes, and he teased me about it!"

"Are you sure that you were not just intoxicated by the handsome man you were with?"

"No!" Rose laughed, thinking at the same time he could have been part her strange feeling.

"No?" Tara said, a grin on her face.

"I really enjoy being with him though," Rose added, taking a cookie from the plate.

"Well, what woman wouldn't? He's the best looking man on the reservation," Tara laughed. "He's quite a catch, you know," she rushed on. "A lot of women have tried to date him, but he hasn't been interested...well, not until you came along."

"Do you mean to tell me he's never dated during all this time that he's been back home?"

"That's right! He has not shown any interest in anyone until you entered the picture, lady!" Tara laughed, then added, "Are you going to see him again?"

"Oh, I don't know," Rose said indifferently, not telling Tara that she couldn't get him out of her mind.

"And why not?"

Rose looked at Tara thoughtfully. "I think he likes me, but...."

"Rose, open your eyes. The man's in love with you!"

"No..."

"Yes! He probably dreams of making you his wife someday," Tara rushed on.

"You see too many romantic movies, Tara."

"No! Listen to me. I've watched him when he's around you. I tell you the man's in love with you. It shows all over his face."

"You're talking crazy."

"Don't you care for him too?"

Rose hesitated, then spoke softly. "Yes...and I really like his family."

"His family?"

"Yes."

Tara laughed. "Well, that's good...'cause he's my cousin!"

"What?"

"Yep! And all of us in the family hope you will date him again...and again!"

"Oh, I don't know," Rose shrugged. "We'll see." She took a bite of cookie and a little smile played across her face. "We'll see."

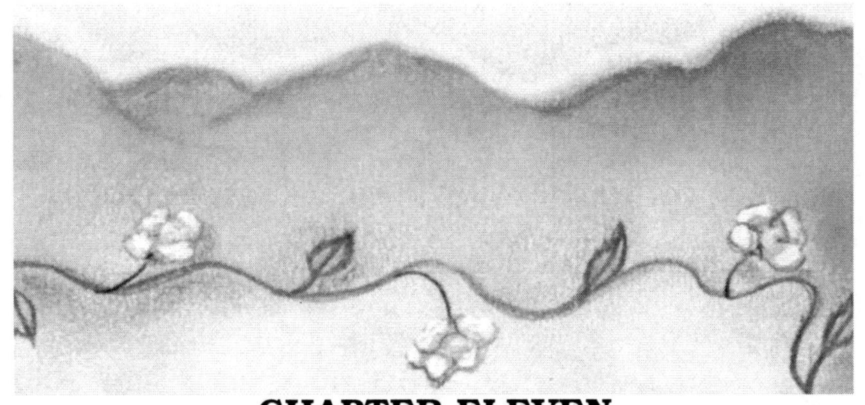

CHAPTER ELEVEN
The White Feather

Rose, I won't be able to see you for a few weeks."

The surprised woman looked at Lone Wolfe quickly. "What?"

"I won't see you for a few weeks," he repeated.

Rose and Lone Wolfe were seeing each other almost every day now and he took her to visit his family often. "Are you going away?" she asked.

"I'm going to my cabin for a while."

"You have a cabin?"

"Yes. It's up in the mountains. It's in a very remote place about fifteen miles from here. It's where I go to write sometimes...with no interruptions. I hope to complete my book by the first of

April...if I have no distractions."

"I see."

Rose tried not to let the disappointment show in her voice for she knew that his going was necessary or he wouldn't leave her. It would be lonely without him.

"It's very quiet up there...no telephone...no neighbors...except for some forest animals," he laughed.

"When are you leaving?"

"Probably tomorrow. I have my supplies and food packed in the truck already."

Lone Wolfe moved closer to Rose. "I will miss you, Rose," he said, looking into her eyes.

"And I will miss you too, Lone Wolfe," she whispered.

He gently pulled Rose to him, wrapped his arms around her, and kissed her. "I hope you will want see my little cabin someday, Rose."

"I would like that," she answered softly before he kissed her again.

"While you are gone," she said suddenly, "do you think Grandpa would mind if I spend some time with him? He is so wise. I want to learn from him."

"He would like that very much." Lone Wolfe smiled at Rose.

Several days later Rose drove out to see Grandpa. She had visited him often since Christmas and a strong bond was developing between them. She appreciated his wisdom and knew that he had experienced much in his long life and she wanted to learn from it.

"Grandpa, I'm so glad to see you," Rose

said, hugging the old man, and then pulled a chair close to him, relishing his company.

Grandpa smiled broadly. He loved her visits and looked forward to them. Recently he had begun teaching her words in the Cherokee language. He had explained to her how important it was for the Cherokee people to preserve their language.

"We must keep our Cherokee language alive," he had said. "If we lose our language we have lost our identity."

Today Rose had come, eager to ask him about the cemetery she had visited with Lone Wolfe. And to tell him about the trip she had made recently.

"Grandpa, Lone Wolfe took me to the Georgia cemetery," she began.

"Yes. He told me."

"Grandpa, there's something I need to tell you...something that happened to me when I went to the cemetery by myself last week. I hope that you can tell me what it means."

The old man looked at Rose and nodded. "I will try...what happened?"

"While I was there I was drawn to the grave that has rocks piled by it." She paused briefly, then continued, "I found a white feather at the foot of the grave. I picked it up and put it in my pocket to save. When I got home it was not in my pocket. I know that I didn't lose it...my pocket was deep. And Grandpa, I know that I didn't imagine it." She leaned closer to Grandpa and looked into his face, searching for an answer. "What does it mean?"

Grandpa had listened carefully to Rose, nodding his head slowly as she explained her experience at the burial grounds.

She waited for him to speak.

Finally he smiled slowly, reached out and took Rose's hand. "The feather was meant just for you, Rose."

"But, what does it mean? What happened to the fea....?"

The old Cherokee held up his hand and stopped her question. "Someday you will understand," he said softly.

Rose was disappointed. She had hoped that Grandpa would explain the meaning of her finding the feather. "But...."

"You must find out for yourself, Rose," he said, patting her hand, "then you will understand."

. "I...guess I understand, Grandpa. I want to know," she said. "And there's something else. While I was at the graveside, Grandpa, I had a strange feeling that has not gone away. It's as if I had been there before...but I know I haven't."

"Someday you will understand," he repeated, smiling at Rose.

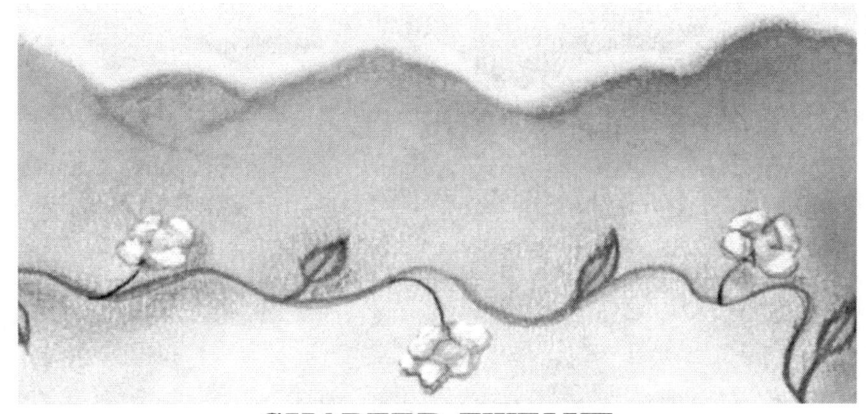

CHAPTER TWELVE

U-ne-ga-U-da-li

A week later Rose went back to talk to Grandpa, eager to tell him about the last trip to Georgia...and to ask him questions.

"Grandpa, I've been back to the cemetery," Rose told the Cherokee elder, hugging him.

"You are lonely without Lone Wolfe around?" he asked.

"Oh, yes. I miss him."

"Is that why you went back to the place in Georgia?"

"Well," Rose said, "it's really sort of...well...I can't explain why I am being drawn back to the burial grounds of people that I don't even know."

Grandpa nodded his head, but did not respond.

"And I am pulled to the grave covered with

rocks. I even dream of standing beside it."

Grandpa nodded again.

"Do you know who is buried there?" she asked, not waiting for an answer. "It looked like the name is worn off."

"Yes...I know."

"Who is it, Grandpa? Please tell me."

"The woman from the grave?"

"Yes!"

He sat quietly, not moving.

"Grandpa?"

He looked into Rose's eyes and said, "It is the grave of U-ne-ga-U-da-li, the Legend Woman."

"The Legend Woman?"

"Yes. She lived over one hundred years ago. When I was a boy I first heard of her from my Grandpa. She was talked about for years and became a legend among the Cherokee people."

"What did she do to become a legend, Grandpa?"

"It all started when the soldiers came and took her and her family away. They lived in a little cabin they built themselves. Looters burned the cabin after they left. She and her husband with their children were on the walk to Oklahoma. Her husband died on the trail. She endured much, but she was always planning to bring her children back to their ancestral home."

Grandpa paused.

Rose pulled her chair closer, not wanting to miss a word. "How did she become a legend?" she asked impatiently, wanting Grandpa to continue the story.

"She was brave."

"What did she do?"

"After the removal was over she found herself two horses...sat her two little children on one horse, settled herself on the other, then rode across the country, determined to come back to their home. She did not know the way. She only had a gold nugget to buy supplies and there were times along the trail when she braved the weather, other Indians, white men, hungry animals, and the rugged country."

Grandpa paused, resting a moment, and then continued.

"Weeks went by...she followed the signs of the forest, of the moon, of the rising and setting sun. Rain washed them, rivers slowed them. Heat almost overcame them, but she came home. When she arrived she found only the chimney left where the looters had burned her cabin. My Grandpa said everyone talked about her because she was so brave...a young mother full of courage."

"Grandpa, what are those rocks by her grave...what does it mean?"

"The rocks are from the chimney of the little cabin. The cabin sat where she is buried."

"And she is called The Legend Woman," Rose said thoughtfully, more to herself than to Grandpa.

"Yes. She was a survivor...a Cherokee determined to overcome all the bad things that happened to her."

"What was her name again, Grandpa?"

"U-ne-ga U-da-li," he answered softly, smiling at Rose. "It means 'White Feather'."

.

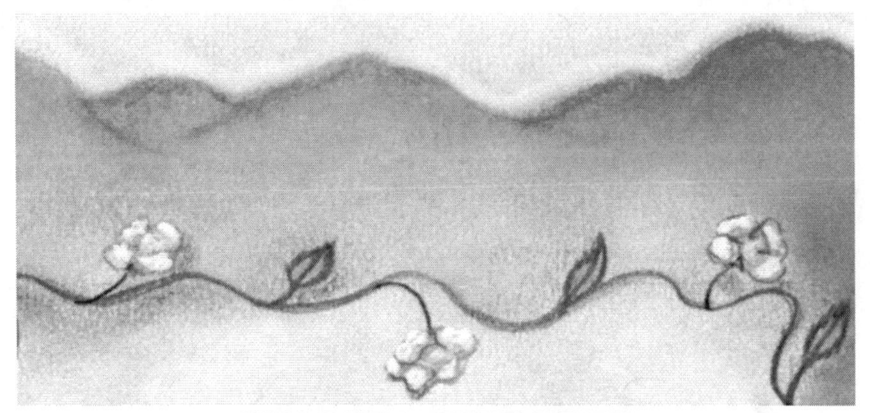

CHAPTER THIRTEEN
Answered Love

Lone Wolfe and Rose rode in silence, enjoying the beauty surrounding them. The truck moved effortlessly through each turn that took them higher into the mountains. Every curve introduced them to a more beautiful view.

"We're almost there," said Lone Wolfe, turning onto a narrow gravel road and looking briefly at Rose. "I told you that my cabin was high on a mountain," he laughed. "Is this narrow road scaring you?"

Rose nodded, shuddered, then laughed. "But I love the view."

She had been thrilled when Lone Wolfe invited her to go to his cabin to spend the afternoon. He had not been since the cold weather had turned to early spring and he had told her he was anxious to see if there was damage to the cabin during the ice and snows of winter.

The truck rounded a sharp curve and a small log cabin snuggled into a cove near the top of the mountain came into view. Sunlight glinted silver from the tin roof of the cabin. A chimney climbed out of the roof on one side. A wooden deck built across the front of the cabin had a swing and several rocking chairs turned and propped against the front wall of the house.

"Oh, Lone Wolfe," Rose whispered in awe, "It's so beautiful."

"I thought you might like it," he said while he parked the truck close to the stone front steps.

"Be careful, Rose. It's very steep here," he warned, opening the truck door for her.

"Yes, it is," she laughed, bracing herself to keep from falling as she stepped out of the truck.

They climbed the steps to the porch, arm in arm, and watched a small squirrel scurry off the deck.

"Looks like I've had company this winter," Lone Wolfe smiled while he unlocked the door.

Stepping inside he motioned for Rose to enter the cabin.

She walked into the dark room and tried to look at its interior.

"I'll have some light in here in just a minute," Lone Wolfe said, moving from window to window raising shades, letting the sunlight flood into the room.

"You'll have to excuse my housekeeping...or lack of it," he laughed. "When I am up here writing I don't do much cleaning."

Rose's gaze swept the room. On one side of the large main room of the house was a huge stone fireplace, occupying almost the entire wall. Wide wooden planks formed the walls and floors, while masculine furniture dominated the comfortable-looking room. Lone Wolfe's writing desk sat against the opposite wall, strewn with papers.

A door from the main room led to a small bedroom with a huge bed occupying most of the space. A chair and floor lamp sat in the corner of the room with a bookcase filled with books nearby. The room also had a small closet.

Rose moved to the kitchen while Lone Wolfe watched her. A table and two chairs were in the middle of the room. The light-colored wooden cabinets had glass doors displaying dishes and various baking pans.

Rose turned and looked at Lone Wolfe. "I like your cabin."

"Thank you."

Walking back into the living room she looked at Lone Wolfe. "Where is the bath...?"

"The bathroom?"

Rose nodded.

"Come here. I will show you."

He took Rose's arm and moved her to the window over the kitchen sink and pointed. "There it is in the back yard," he said, watching Rose's reaction in amusement.

"Oh, dear!" she exclaimed.

"You are in a primitive cabin, my dear," he teased.

"I see."

"I come here mainly to write or paint, away from everybody and everything. I don't use the cabin very often, but it's comfortable for me. I have a wood stove. I keep plenty of can goods here and the spring is nearby for water. Occasionally I hunt and fish. The river is not too far from here. You can see it from the front deck." He paused and watched while Rose continued to look around. "Well, what do you think of my little get-away?"

"I love it. I can see why you like it here." Looking out the window at the view of the mountains, she asked, "Tell me, do you ever see bears up here?"

"Sure...when they smell food. If I'm cooking or carrying food I am watchful and cautious. If they're hungry, bears might attack...but not often."

"Oh," Rose said, nervously looking out the window.

"Don't be afraid," Lone Wolfe said, putting his arm around Rose's shoulders. "It's all right. We have no food with us, so they won't care if we are here. Come on, let's go out on the porch."

Rose walked to the edge of the deck and leaned on the banister. "It's so pretty," she said. "The view is breathtaking." She breathed deeply of the fresh mountain air. "Umm. I love it."

"I thought that you would like it," Lone Wolfe said. "Do you see the Rock Face on the side of the mountain?"

"Where?"

"On that tall mountain over there," Lone Wolfe said, pointing to the formation.

"Oh yes, now I see it," said Rose. "I imagine that it can be seen for miles."

"Seems that way, but actually you get the best view of it from the river."

"It's very unusual."

"Enjoy the scenery while I check around the cabin to see if anything has received winter damage. I'll be right back."

Rose turned and watched Lone Wolfe walk away, his hair blowing in the gentle breeze. He wore his dark hair long, parted down the middle. Sometimes it fell loose around his shoulders, but was usually gathered and tied in the back with narrow strips of deer leather. Today he wore it down and Rose loved the way the wind played with it, blowing the strands over his shoulders. It reminded her of the evening she had declared her love for him. Quietly, there on the deck, Rose's thoughts easily slipped back to that evening....

The smell of honeysuckle had floated about their heads as a soft breeze stirred the softness of his loosened hair. The movement of it held her gaze while the sweetness of the evening opened her heart. The essence of him had been there waiting to slip through the innocence of her love. Once inside, her heart leapt with emotions she had never known before.

"He is my heart...I must tell him."

And then, as the words fell from her lips as softly as a feather falls, the strong hand of the Cherokee reached out and opened the pathway to his heart to catch them within the depth of answered love.

Lost in her thoughts of how much she loved Lone Wolfe she did not hear him return a short time later. She jumped slightly when he put his arms around her waist and turned her to him.

"You are so beautiful," Lone Wolfe said. He

kissed her slowly, then passionately while he whispered his love for her between kisses.

She cradled her head in the crook of his shoulder. “I love it here, Lone Wolfe,” she said softly, “can we stay for the rest of the day?”

“Yes,” he smiled and then led her into the cabin.

Later the headlights on the truck lit the narrow road that led down the mountain away from the cabin.

Rose rested within the arc of Lone Wolfe’s arm while she slept.

Lone Wolfe smiled, thinking how great his love had become for this woman. He knew that he had truly found his treasure.

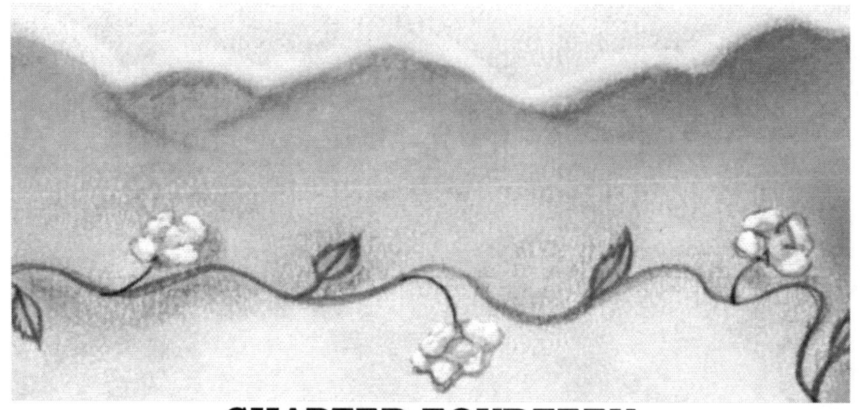

CHAPTER FOURTEEN

Not Alone

Rose was excited. She had gotten out of bed early, eager to get to the Georgia cemetery. Now that she knew who was buried in the grave with the stones beside it she was anxious to go back to the grave of White Feather, The Legend Woman.

Arriving at the cemetery she hurried up the hill. Upon reaching White Feather's grave she paused, almost breathless. She stood for a moment and then dropped to her knees and opened the bag she had brought with her. She took out heavy work gloves and slipped them on her hands, then leaned over and began to rub the rock where part of the name appeared. Rubbing hard she soon uncovered U-ne-ga U-da-li, then resumed trying to uncover the remaining letters hidden by the dirt and debris of time. Finally she saw the name. She leaned back and read slowly, "White Feather..." letting the sound of the name rise gently into the warm air.

She took off her gloves and caressed the name with her fingertips, then stood and looked at the grave. An unusual feeling moved through her body and she looked around quickly, feeling that she was not alone. She saw no one. She turned back and faced the grave. Again a soft and gentle feeling of someone near flowed through her body. She was not afraid, instead she welcomed the feeling. Strangely she felt the urge to wrap her arms around her body and look up at the mountains.

Around and around Rose turned, slowly guiding her footsteps in small pirouettes, gazing at the panoramic view of the majestic hazy blue-green mountains surrounding her. Contentedly she listened.

The breeze brought the flutter of leaves...songs of birds floated from the nearby trees. Listening she could hear the water dancing gently over the rocks in the river across the road. Now she stood perfectly still, looking at the mountains, allowing the music to stimulate her senses. Her gaze embraced the distant mountains. The sights and sounds warmed Rose's heart.

How White Feather must have loved living here, she thought.

She turned and went to the pile of rocks near the grave. Slowly she ran her fingers across a large stone. It excited her to think that White Feather might have touched the same rock that she now caressed. Reaching down she picked up a small stone and slipped it into her pocket, knowing that she would think of White Feather each time she looked at it.

Turning away from the grave and looking around, she again felt that she was not alone, but she saw no one...and her thoughts returned to The Legend Woman.

White Feather came home to this land she loved so much. Nothing has changed. This quiet secluded place is so beautiful and peaceful. I would love to live here also.

"I am seeing the same land that she saw," Rose whispered, smiling. "Maybe I can speak to her."

With her heart in her throat, the anxious woman raised her eyes skyward. Her voice, trembling with emotion, eased into the clearing.

"White Feather...I can feel your presence. I understand why you came all the way across this land to return home. All around the beauty spreads out. It seeps into every pore of the body. When I go away, there's a gentle deep-down yearning to come back. Please, may I share this place with you? May I call this my home also?"

Rose's voice died to the strands of the windsong whirling through the trees. She glanced up just as warmth entered her body...a feeling she'd never experienced before. It engulfed her with happiness and fed her spirit. Her hair spread out into the breeze and Rose knew she had been accepted...that she could now call these mountains her home.

"Grandpa, I went to White Feather's grave yesterday."

"You did?" he said, smiling.

Rose had come to see Grandpa, eager to tell him about her trip and about something she had found while she was there.

"Yes. I cleaned off the grave marker and now you can see her name."

The old man nodded, pleased. "That is good."

"Grandpa, I saw a thorny small bush growing beside White Feather's grave. It had little green leaves that made it look like a small rose bush. I started to pull it up but then I thought I would ask you first since it was so near White Feather's grave."

"Do not pull it up. I know about it. It is a flower."

"A flower?"

"Yes. It has been there for many, many years. One of White Feather's descendants planted it. It is called a Cherokee Rose."

Rose moved closer to Grandpa. "A Cherokee Rose?"

"Yes. It will have beautiful blooms on it soon."

"Oh...what will they look like?"

"Have you ever heard about the Cherokee Rose bush?"

"No."

Grandpa straightened himself, cleared his throat and began.

"There's a story the Cherokee tell...it had to do with pain and suffering. It all happend when our people were driven out of their homes in Georgia...over one hundred years ago. One of the reasons was that gold was discovered on their lands. The Cherokee people named the journey 'The Trail Where They Cried'." Grandpa paused and looked at Rose.

She nodded.

"It was a bad time for the Cherokee. Many died from hardships and the women cried. The elders knew that the women must be strong and take care of their children so that the little ones would survive. So the old men called upon the Creator to help their people and to give the mothers strength. The Great One caused a plant to spring up everywhere a mother's tear had fallen to the ground on their journey. He told the old men that the plant would grow quickly, then fall back to the ground and another plant would grow."

Grandpa rested his voice for a moment, cleared his throat and then continued.

"The plant would have white blossoms...a beautiful rose with five petals and gold in the center to represent the gold taken from Cherokee lands. It would have seven green leaves on each stem, one for each Cherokee Clan. It would be strong and grow quickly throughout the land all along the Trail of Tears. The stickers on the stem would protect it from anyone who might try to move it."

Grandpa looked at Rose, then continued.

"The next morning the women saw the beautiful white flowers far back on the trail. When they heard what the Great One had said, they felt strong and knew that they would survive. They took care of their children, knowing that they would grow and be strong also. The wild Cherokee Rose grows along the route of the Trail of Tears all the way into eastern Oklahoma today."

When he finished the story Grandpa looked at Rose and smiled. "It's a very beautiful flower."

"That's a wonderful story, Grandpa. Did you say that it grows wild?"

"Yes, but many people plant them in their yards."

"I can hardly wait to see it blossom."

"There are many different kinds of plants that grow wild around here...some you can eat."

"There are?"

"Yes...and flowers too." He looked at Rose and smiled. "Have you seen the little purple violets that are blooming now?"

Rose nodded. "Yes. They are everywhere. Can you eat them?" she asked in surprise.

Grandpa nodded. "Yes. There are others too. But some are poison that can....."

Suddenly the front door burst open, interrupting Grandpa.

"Hello! I'm home!" Lone Wolfe shouted as he entered the room.

Rose turned, hearing the sound of his voice, leapt up and quickly ran into his arms.

Grandpa chuckled. Watching the scene between the two young people he nodded and whispered. "Lone Wolfe needs to be happy. Rose needs to be happy. Neither should be alone."

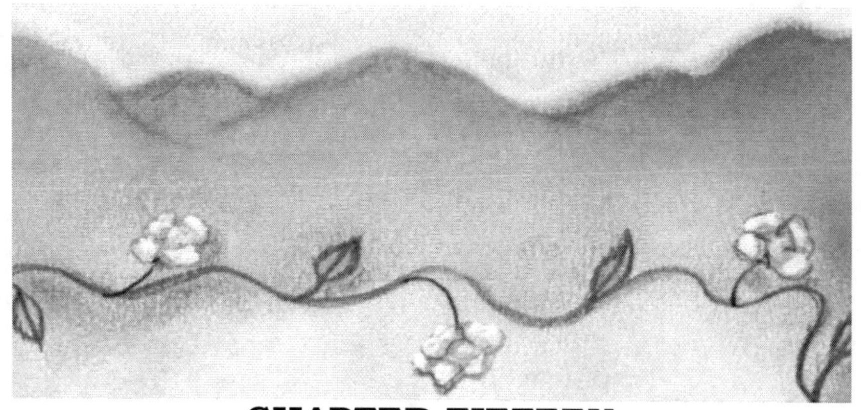

CHAPTER FIFTEEN

Clem

On Thursday afternoon Lone Wolfe whistled happily as he drove toward his cabin making plans of preparation for Rose's visit. It was spring and all the flowers were in full bloom...a beautiful time of the year to be at his cabin. He was looking forward to Rose's arrival. He had planned a very special surprise for her...one he hoped would bring a smile to her face. He reached the cabin during the early afternoon.

While Lone Wolfe unloaded the boxes of food and supplies from his truck hidden eyes watched his every move. The lone shadow crouched, engulfed by the large tree trunk, unseen by Lone Wolfe on his trips in and out of the cabin.

Remembering that the nights were still cool Lone Wolfe looked at the wood stacked on the deck and decided that he needed more for the weekend knowing how Rose enjoyed a fire in the fireplace. He went to the wood pile behind the cabin and brought several loads to the deck. When he finished he opened the cabin door and went inside.

The last thing he remembered was the stabbing pain on the back of his head as he pitched toward the floor and into darkness.

When Lone Wolfe slowly opened his eyes he tried to hold up his head. His dimmed gaze traveled across the floor to a pair of hiking boots and then upward, stopping at the face of a stranger, a man wearing clothes and boots from Lone Wolfe's closet.

"Well, it's about time you came to," the man laughed, looking at Lone Wolfe with beady eyes. "I thought I had dang near killed you."

Lone Wolfe raised his head slightly and tried to pull himself up off the floor. The throbbing pain in his head caused him to fall back.

"I thought you was out for good...you been asleep so long," the unfamiliar voice boomed out.

Lone Wolfe tried to move again, but his hands were tied behind his back and his feet were tightly bound together.

"Untie me."

"Naw, ain't gonna do it," the intruder said, scratching the new growth of beard, his face twisting to the side.

"This is my house. What are you doing here?" Lone Wolfe said, trying to look up at the man. "Who are you?"

"Nobody you know! It looks like I'm in charge of your house now, don't it?" he laughed.

"Where did you come from?" Lone Wolfe asked, remembering that he had seen no vehicle outside.

"You ain't got to know," he sneered, his eyes narrowing, looking at Lone Wolfe.

"Untie me!" Lone Wolfe demanded, struggling to stand. Picking up Lone Wolfe's pistol that he had found while pilfering through the desk, he waved it at Lone Wolfe.

"You talk too much!" he said while walking to Lone Wolfe. "I'm tired of your mouth!" He struck Lone Wolfe on the head with the pistol handle.

Again Lone Wolfe saw darkness and lay unmoving on the floor.

Early morning sunlight streaming through the window woke Lone Wolfe. He opened his eyes slightly, and saw that he was now lying on the floor in the bedroom. His head throbbed with pain. His body tingled with numbness and stiffness from not being able to move. He was thirsty and hungry and could smell food. When he tried to rise he fell back on the floor too weak to stand. He rolled his body over so that he could see into the kitchen.

The man sat at the table eating. Hearing the movement, he got up and came to the bedroom with the pistol in his hand.

"Are you hungry?"

"Yes," Lone Wolfe answered weakly.

"Well, since I'm a kindly feller, I'm gonna let you eat a little, but don't try nothing," he said. "If you do I'm gonna use this gun and it'll be for more than just hitting you with it...you got that?" He gave Lone Wolfe a vicious kick.

Lone Wolfe, still blinking back the pain of the kick, nodded.

The intruder went back to the kitchen and picked up a plate of food from the table. He put it on the floor and shoved it toward Lone Wolfe with his foot. Only then did he untie Lone Wolfe's hands.

When the slightly recovering man had finished eating he looked toward his captor and said, "I need to go outside."

"All right, but I'll be right behind you with this gun so don't try nothing," he said, waving the gun in Lone Wolfe's face. Kneeling, the grizzled man then untied his feet. Standing, he jerked Lone Wolfe up onto his numb, shaky legs.

"Who are you?" Lone Wolfe questioned as they went outside.

"You can call me Clem," he growled at Lone Wolfe.

When the men returned to the cabin Clem tied Lone Wolfe's hands once again behind his back...tighter than before. He pushed him into the bedroom and down on the floor, retied his feet, then left the room.

Lone Wolfe struggled with the ropes but they were on his body so tightly that they cut into his skin. When he struggled to sit up he could feel blood running down the back of his head and into his collar. His head swam and he almost passed out. He could see the man eating again, food that he had brought from the truck, food that he had planned to serve Rose when she arrived tomorrow afternoon...or was it today? He had lost track.

Rose...Rose...Rose, he thought. He couldn't let her come into this situation. He hoped she would not come, but then he realized that he was not thinking clearly. He knew that she would arrive today. Yes, today...that was right...they had been planning this weekend for a month. He struggled with the rope that held him tight; groping with swollen fingers he tried to pull at it. Nothing...he could do nothing. He moaned.

About dusk Clem rushed into the bedroom. "Sit up!" he ordered Lone Wolfe, kicking him with his foot.

Holding the wide tape he had found in the desk drawer, he stretched out a piece and slapped it across Lone Wolfe's mouth.

"Someone's coming up the mountain and I want you to be quiet," he said, pushing Lone Wolfe completely out of sight under the bed.

"Don't you make a noise now, you hear? I've still got this gun!"

Lone Wolfe heard the door close as weakness and loss of blood overtook him and he drifted back into unconsciousness. He never heard Rose call his name, over and over.

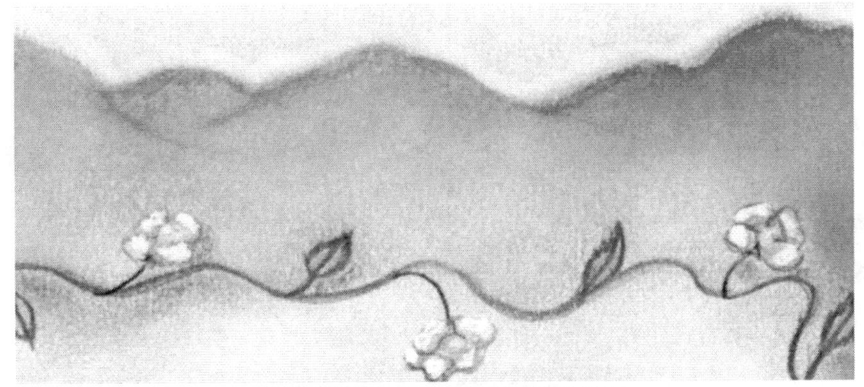

CHAPTER SIXTEEN
Hostage

Rose was anxious to get to the cabin. She had looked forward to the weekend for days. Lone Wolfe had left the day before.

Turning the final curve in the road the cabin came into view. She smiled when she noticed the curling trail of smoke slowly rising from the stone chimney, pleased that Lone Wolfe remembered how much she enjoyed an open fire. She could hardly wait to get inside. The nights were growing cooler with the fall season coming soon and she would enjoy sitting in front of the fireplace tonight.

She parked her van next to Lone Wolfe's truck and jumped out, eager to see him. Racing up the steps she burst into the living room, planning to surprise him with her arrival.

"Lone Wolfe! Lone Wolfe!" she called, pausing in the living room. "Lone Wolfe!" she called louder, walking to the bedroom door and opened it thinking he might be taking a nap. Not finding him there, she stopped her search, deciding that he was in the woods.

Rose went back to her van to bring in her bags. Behind a nearby tree, Clem watched her every move. He stood silently, waiting.

When Rose returned to the van and leaned over the seat to retrieve her last bag, hands grabbed her from behind.

She screamed!

"Shut up!" A voice snarled, pinning her hands behind her back. "Get in the house!"

Rose could not see the face of her captor and each time she tried to look behind her the hands twisted her arms tighter, causing pain to travel up her shoulders. When they entered the cabin the hands released her, pushing Rose forward, causing her to fall to the floor. Frightened she looked at the man and then quickly glanced around the room for Lone Wolfe.

"Lone Wolfe! Lone Wolfe!" she screamed.

"Shut up! He ain't gonna answer you!"

"Where is he?" Rose cried out. "What have you done with him?"

"He's around," Clem laughed loudly.

"Lone Wolfe!" she cried, looking around the room while struggling to a sitting position.

Clem pulled on her arm. "Get up off the floor. Get up and sit down in this chair," he ordered, then walked over to a chair and pushed it toward her with his foot.

"No!"

She stood, ran to the man and flew into him with both fists while he laughed at her efforts. Grabbing her shoulders, he pushed her down in the chair and tied her hands behind her and bound her feet together.

Rose tried to kick him but he stepped away and laughed.

"Boy, ain't you a wild one! And pretty too," he added, patting her on the head.

Rose watched Clem go into the bedroom. She heard a noise in the room but could not see what he was doing.

Inside the bedroom, Clem pulled Lone Wolfe from under the bed and stripped the tape from his mouth.

"Get up!" he demanded, pulling Lone Wolfe to his feet, then almost dragged him toward the living room. Once there, he pushed him back onto the floor. "We got company!"

Rose screamed when she saw Lone Wolfe hobble into the room and struggled to release herself to go to him.

"Rose, I'll kill him if he harms you...I promise," Lone Wolfe said weakly, watching Clem walk out the front door.

"Who is he?" Rose asked.

"I don't know. He was in the cabin when I got here yesterday," Lone Wolfe said, turning his head to look toward the door.

Rose gasped when she saw the back of his head! "Lone Wolfe! You're hurt...your head has been bleeding!" Rose said, seeing the dried blood on his shirt and neck.

"Yes."

The door opened and Clem entered the

room, then slammed the door.

He sat down heavily in a chair and eyed both of his prisoners. "Well, I was gonna use you," he said, pointing to Lone Wolfe, "but I think I'm gonna take her. I think she'll be more fun,"

"NO!" yelled Lone Wolfe. "Leave her alone!"

"Take me where?" Rose asked, fear in her voice.

Clem rose and walked over to Rose. "We're gonna leave here in the morning and you're gonna buy my way to freedom...my hostage...my pretty little hostage." He grinned at Rose and ran his hand roughly under her chin.

"No!" Lone Wolfe shouted, struggling to release himself, his wrists bleeding from the ropes cutting into them.

"Oh yeah. We're gonna walk right out of these mountains...ain't nobody gonna stop us! And we can even have some fun on the way out," he said, winking at Rose.

Early the next morning Clem took Lone Wolfe and then Rose outside to the little back building, walking behind them on each trip, pointing the pistol to their backs. Afterwards he untied their hands and gave each of them a small amount of food to eat, guarding them again with the pistol while they ate.

The pair watched silently while the intruder took Lone Wolfe's backpack and filled it with what was left of Lone Wolfe's stash. He stuffed the backpack as full as space allowed, then slung it over his back. He picked up the pistol from the table and untied Rose while Lone Wolfe struggled desperately to loosen himself.

"Leave her alone!" Lone Wolfe shouted.

"Aw, just shut up!" Clem bellowed back at Lone Wolfe, waving the gun toward him.

As soon as Rose's feet were untied she began kicking Clem, landing blows wherever her feet could reach.

"You sure got a lot of spunk! I like that!" Clem grinned. "I was gonna untie you but looks like I need to keep your hands tied up. Come on, we're leaving," he said, roughly pulling Rose to her feet.

Lone Wolfe continued struggling to free himself, blood from his wrists now running down into his hands while Clem laughed at him.

"Come on! Let's go!" he ordered, pushing Rose from behind.

"I'm not going anywhere with you," Rose said, running to Lone Wolfe's side.

Clem grabbed Rose by the arm and pulled her roughly to him. "Well, we'll be seeing you...or maybe not!" he laughed, looking at Lone Wolfe.

"NO!" Lone Wolfe yelled. "Leave her here. Take me!"

"Don't want you now! She's going!"

"NO!"

"I'm tired of listening to you," he said cruelly, then struck Lone Wolfe on the head with the pistol.

"Lone Wolfe!" Rose screamed, watching him pitch forward onto the floor, blood oozing from another head wound. She called his name again, tears streaming down her face.

Lone Wolfe did not move.

Rose tried to run to him, but Clem caught her by the hair, yanking her toward the door.

"Come on, girl," he said, and dragged the protesting woman through the door, away from Lone Wolfe.

Looking back over her shoulder Rose saw that he had not moved. Is he dead? she thought in terror. She couldn't tell...he was so still...not moving.

Hot tears rolled down her face while she stumbled blindly down the steps, imprisoned by a man she had never seen before...while the man she loved was left lying silently on the floor of the little cabin.

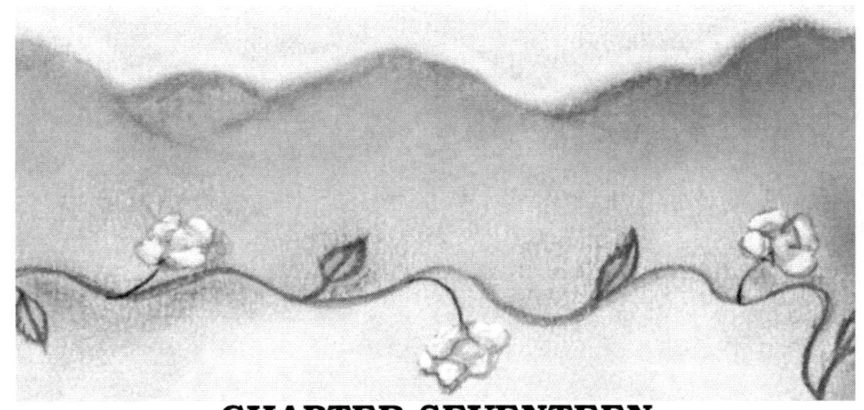

CHAPTER SEVENTEEN

A Way to Freedom

Clem opened the door to Lone Wolfe's truck, shoved Rose down on the seat and slammed the door. While he walked around to the other side of the truck Rose attempted to open the door of the vehicle, but her hands were tied too tightly. He got in and noisily slammed the door and put the backpack on the seat between them.

"Where's the keys?" Clem glared at Rose when he saw that they were not in the ignition.

"I don't know," she answered.

"I said...where's the keys?" he yelled.

"I don't know," she repeated, then added, "...probably in Lone Wolfe's pocket."

"It don't matter. We'll just use your van," he said, not wanting to take the time to return to the cabin.

Clem jerked Rose out of the truck and she fell on the ground, hurting her knees.

Roughly he pulled her up and they went to the van. She glanced toward the cabin, hoping to see a recovered Lone Wolfe coming to save her. Tears once more began to stream down her face.

"Get in there," her captor ordered, pushing Rose into the van.

She frowned, remembering that she had left the keys in the ignition and wishing that she had taken them out when she arrived. While Clem walked to the other side of the van Rose tried to open the inside door with her bound hands.

"What do you think you're doing? You stop that! You ain't going nowhere," Clem said, glaring at Rose when he sat down next to her.

Backing the van, he turned it around and drove down the gravel road.

They traveled several miles. Rose, watching Clem, felt sure that he had no idea where he was headed. She didn't either, she only knew that the road was taking her away from Lone Wolfe.

I must do something to stop the van, she thought. With all the strength she could gather she leaned across the backpack and lunged against Clem, causing him to lose control of the van. It veered off the road, rolled down a shallow embankment and lodged in a ditch, completely hiding the van from the road.

Neither of them was hurt, but Rose's action had infuriated Clem and he tried to get the van out of the ditch. "Look what you done!" he yelled at Rose and then slapped her across the face.

He slung the backpack across his shoulder, pulled Rose out of the van, and taking the pistol from his pocket he waved it in her face. "Now we gotta walk!" He pushed Rose. "Get going!"

"How can I walk with my feet tied?"

"You can walk!" Clem began yelling at her. "Come on, you're too slow!"

"I can't walk any faster. I'm doing the best I can."

"Well, we gotta go faster than this."

"I can't!"

"I'm gonna untie your feet, but don't you try nothing, you hear?" he said, shaking her by the shoulders.

Around noon they stopped briefly to rest and eat food from the backpack.

Shoving a piece of bread and a slab of ham to Rose, Clem forgot his anger for a moment, and said, "My name's Clem. What's your name?"

Rose did not respond, instead she stared at him and took a bite of food.

Rose had no idea where they were except she knew that the river was nearby...she could hear water rushing over the rocks. Following the sound of the river they continued their journey through rough terrain, with Clem pulling Rose behind him. The path ended and now the trees and undergrowth were so thick that Rose could barely see in front of her at times. If she slowed her pace Clem would shout obscenities at her and push her forward in front of him.

"We gonna get out of here...to my freedom," he said. "Now get!"

Mid afternoon Clem stopped. "I'm thirsty," he bellowed, seeing the river come into view at the last turn they made in the woods. "We'll stop here."

Rose was thirsty too...and tired, very tired. She sank down on the river's bank and cupped her hand in the water and brought it to her mouth, then splashed the cold water over her face, hoping to find extra strength in its coldness. She raised her head and movement across the river caught her attention. She gasped...frozen in terror!

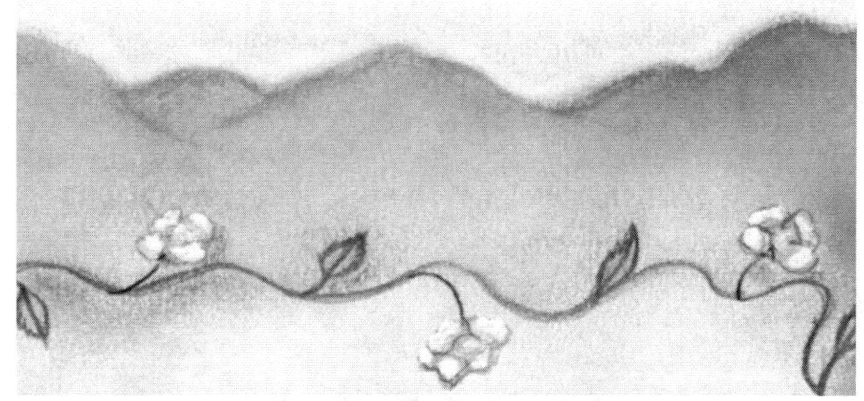

CHAPTER EIGHTEEN

Screams of Death

Across the river, a large black bear had made its way to the edge of the river and had stopped to drink water. Pausing, he held up his head, sniffed the air and resumed drinking. Again lifting his head he sniffed loudly. Smelling the food that Clem carried on his back, the animal started wading across the shallow river...toward Clem and Rose.

Clem did not see the bear until the animal had almost made it across the river.

"A bear! Run!" he shouted to Rose. "It's a bear!" He aimed the pistol toward the bear and shot. The bullet didn't stop the animal; instead, the bear began to pick up speed, water splashing high in his efforts to get to Clem.

Just at the moment when Rose stood to try

to escape, the bear ran past her, brushing her shoulder as it headed for it's prey.

When the bear reached Clem, it lunged toward him and knocked the gun from his hand.

Rose turned and ran in the opposite direction into the woods. She could hear Clem's screams as the bear attacked him. She covered her ears with her hands while the screams of death echoed through the quiet woods. Rose ran blindly, the terrifying cries of pain pushing her further and further away. Sickened by the sound, she forsook any thought except to get away, afraid that the bear might come after her also. She stumbled, caught herself, then increased her speed as she tore through the woods with tree limbs and branches scratching and slicing into her arms as she sped away from the river.

Stopping to catch her breath she eased one hand away from her ears and realized that the screams had become softer...and finally were heard no more. She caught her breath and began to run again. When she turned to glance back she slipped on a tree root protruding from the forest floor and fell. She felt a hot pain searing through her ankle. Attempting to stand she grimaced in pain. Her hand went quickly to her foot, rubbing her ankle. Already it was swelling and she knew that dark bruises would come later.

Still in dreaded fear, she pulled herself up and tried to run again, but the pain in her foot prevented it. A few steps later, everything became dark and she lost consciousness.

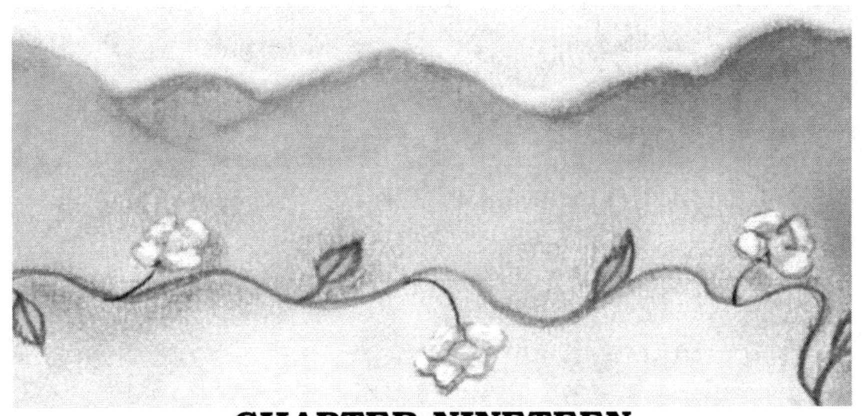

CHAPTER NINETEEN

Lost in the Woods

Early morning sunlight filtered through the trees, covering Rose's face with its warmth, waking her from sleep. She blinked and opened her eyes to look upward. Squinting from the brightness of the sun she realized that she had slept on the ground all night. She had dreamed of Grandpa during the night, but she couldn't remember much about the dream except that he had told her to get up and find the river.

She slowly raised her body from the ground to a sitting position. Grimacing from the pain in her body she uttered a moan. She sat looking around, always watchful for the bear, for any and all bears. She couldn't believe that she had slept all night, then she remembered all that had happened the day before—the miles of walking, the bear and Clem. Shuddering at the remembrance of the bear attack, the spent woman tried to stand, but her swollen and bruised ankle ached from the injury. She sat for a moment, then after several attempts she was able to raise herself to her feet. Looking around for something to support her labored walking she spied a broken limb lying on the ground nearby. She hobbled over to the stick and picked it up, deciding that it would make a good support to help her walk.

Weakly she moved only a few steps but then had to stop and rest. Sitting on the ground she thought about Lone Wolfe.

I must get back to him. If I can find the river again, I will follow it and it will lead back to the cabin, but which way leads to the river? She wondered, her gaze moving over her surroundings.

She stood up, leaned on the stick and trudged through the woods, tired and weak from hunger. Suddenly she stopped. Something red caught her eye and she moved slowly toward it. There, before her, stood a bush heavy with berries. Reaching down, she quickly picked a handful of the ripe berries. But as Rose drew them near her mouth, she remembered Grandpa's words.

"Some berries in the woods are good to eat, but some are poisonous. Never eat any of them unless you know what kind they are...or mushrooms either," he had warned her during one of their long visits together.

Rose let the berries slowly trickle through her fingers and watched them fall to the ground.

"I won't think about eating," she whispered.

"I will only think about getting back to the cabin and helping Lone Wolfe. I will not die lost out here in these woods...I will survive." She determinedly limped forward.

Lone Wolfe...she had to return to him. Horror filled her mind with fear at her last sight of him. Clem had struck him very hard on the head. He might be dead. NO! He could not be dead! She would find her way back to him and get help.

Stopping often to rest, she listened for the sound of the river. She was sure that the river would lead her back to the cabin.

Night was fast approaching. When the sun went down behind the mountains the temperature dropped and Rose grew cold. The stars decorated the sky and soon the full moon appeared, helping to light the dark woods.

Finally, Rose could travel no further. Exhausted, she shivered violently from the cold air now filtering through the woods. She sank down beside the base of a large oak tree where a mound of dead leaves nested against its trunk. She leaned over and began gathering them around her, forming a make-shift bed for herself. She lay down on them, and then pulled the leaves on top of her to form a blanket against the cold night air.

Wearily, she drifted into sleep.

Strangely, all around the sleeping woman, a stillness eased into the area. Night sounds ceased. A small breeze shifted the leaves covering Rose, almost as if a mother's hand smoothed her coverlet. It lasted only for a moment, and then traveled up the trunk into the tender green leaves of spring, playing with the branches, humming harmony with the earth and its vegetation.

The hoot of an owl signaled an all clear as the tall oak stood guard.

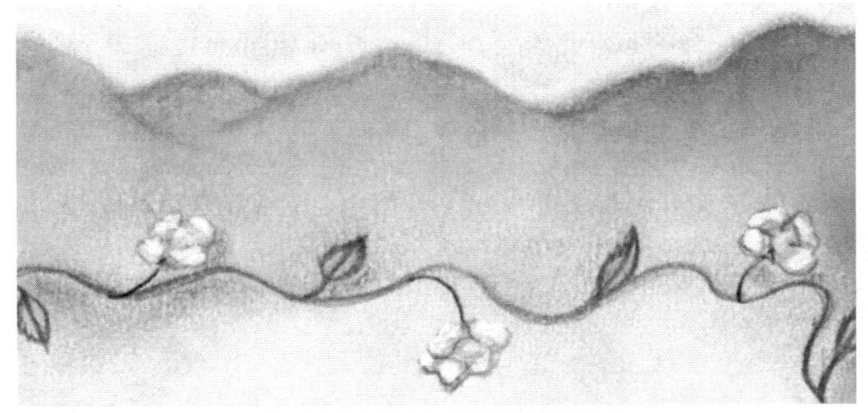

CHAPTER TWENTY
Predators of the Dark

Rose felt that she had been walking for days. Movement was slower now as her ankle had swollen to twice its normal size and she wondered if there could be a broken bone in her foot. She continued to limp along, not daring to speak aloud or make unnecessary noise.

Constantly on the alert for bears, she remembered what had happened at the river and shuddered. Does anyone know that I am lost? she thought. And poor Lone Wolfe...what about him? She sighed. How I long for the comfort of our arms around each other she continued her silent monologue.

Rose pushed on through the forest. When she came to a large fallen tree she sat on its trunk to rest, propping her injured foot up on the log.

Suddenly she heard a thrashing sound nearby piercing the quietness of the woods. She looked up and froze. A large bear was moving slowly toward her, its head down searching the ground for food. The breeze brought the odor of him full upon her face. She sat still for a moment, and then eased herself up. The bear had not seen her and Rose made her way to a tree and tried to conceal herself behind the large trunk.

Quietly, Rose slipped from tree to tree away from the bear. Her heart pounded rapidly. She was sure that the bear would hear it and find her hiding place. When the animal turned, moved away and disappeared, Rose sank to the ground trembling and rubbed her aching foot. She was exhausted and hungry. She put her hand on her grumbling stomach.

"I am so hungry," she whispered softly, nodding and then falling into a much-needed sleep. Once again she dreamed of Grandpa and a recent visit with him.

Rose sat on the floor at Grandpa's feet, looked into his aged face and asked, "Grandpa, what are ramps?"

"Something good to eat," he chuckled. "Lone Wolfe left this morning with a group of men to gather the greens to contribute to the Ramp Day Celebration this weekend."

"I have never heard of ramps before."

"They are plants that grow in shady places on the reservation. They are usually found near water. They're hard to find sometimes."

"And they're good to eat?"

"Oh yes, very tasty, especially if they are

cooked with eggs or potatoes."

"I can't wait to try them."

Grandpa laughed softly. "They have a very strong odor," he said. "My wife used to cook them outside so the house wouldn't smell bad."

"And they're good to eat?"

"Yes."

Drops of water fell on Rose's face, waking her. She looked up into the sky and could see that it was filled with dark rain clouds. She knew how mountain showers could come suddenly and leave just as quickly as they appeared and she hoped that this was one of those times.

I must find shelter she thought. She sat up quickly, crying out in pain. Looking down she saw that the swelling in her foot had increased and red streaks had made their way up to her knee. Struggling she managed to rise. A slight wind blew over her body and damp clothes, chilling her. She moved through the mud to a tree and tried to find shelter under it but now the rain was lashing the trees, falling in torrents and the wind had become stronger. Each gust of wind whipped across Rose, causing her to tremble.

A sharp streak of lightning lit up the sky followed by a loud clap of thunder.

The approaching storm came fast and Rose limped forward seeking a place to find protection from the rain pounding her body. The wind was cold and she was shivering uncontrollably. She knew that when dark came visibility would be reduced to nothing.

Feeling her way along a mountain rock wall she finally found an overhang forming a small cave. Entering cautiously, she felt her way along the cave wall. The inside of the cave was dark but Rose did not care, relieved to be out of the storm...she had found cover for her weary body. She went back to the entrance of the cave, cupped her hand and held it out in the rain to catch water to drink. After she had her fill she turned and went further into the cave.

The cave reeked of stagnant water, seemingly coming from its darkened corners. Animals had recently inhabited the cave, leaving bones of their prey scattered about on the wet floor. The stale air of the cave left a sticky feeling on Rose's arms.

When her eyes became accustomed to the dim light of the cave, she looked around in search of animals, especially a bear which might be crouched in a corner waiting to pounce upon her. Seeing no animals she then searched for a dry place to rest.

Suddenly bats flew into the cave, barely missing Rose's head as they also searched for a place to spend the night. Rose waved her stick around in the air frightening the bats as she herded them outside.

She sat down heavily, rubbed her aching ankle, then leaned back against the cave wall and closed her eyes, once again exhausted. In less than a minute she was asleep.

Rose had not slept long when she awoke with a start, hearing a noise close by.

The rain had stopped and most of the clouds had moved on. She strained her eyes, trying to see out into the darkness. Trembling, she sat up and leaned forward, attempting to see into the quiet forest.

She heard the crunching sound again...and then again. The sound on the wet grass came nearer.

Her hand quietly scanned the ground beside her, hoping to find a stray rock to use for a weapon. She found nothing.

A cloud covering the full moon slipped on and moonlight lit the outside of the cave.

Rose gasped.

A wolf stood not fifteen feet away from the cave entrance, staring into the darkness of the cave. Rose shrunk back against the wall, hoping that the wolf had not heard nor seen her. She was sure the animal could hear her heart beating rapidly, loudly pulsating in her ears. She did not move.

The cry of his mate in the woods nearby drew the attention of the wolf. He turned and followed the sound, leaving Rose panting for breath.

Tears of frustration streamed down her face as she lifted her gaze in the darkness while praying for courage and guidance.

While sleep finally overcame her fear she was sure she heard a soft soothing voice about her head.

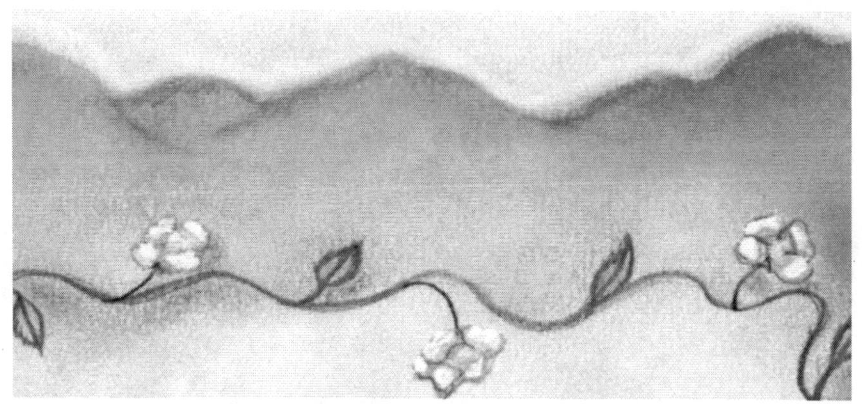

CHAPTER TWENTY-ONE

Rose's Protector

When Rose awoke after a restless night of sleep she hobbled to the opening of the cave and looked out. Heavy fog covered everything. She could not see into the woods and decided that it would be useless to try to find the river now so she sank down on the cave floor and drifted back into sleep.

Her dreams this time came slowly, dimly. She could see herself kneeling in the fog...but there was someone else close to her, someone with arms lifted as if in homage to the Protector. The woman's hair was spread out all around her in a dark cloud. She was singing, singing over Rose's head. Rose felt the woman's voice cloaking her body like spun honey.

"Squah-tee-she-sdee, Yee-ho-wah,
El-lah-dee-suh-ee
Jee-wah-nah-lee-yoo-ah-yuh
Jah-lee-nee-gee-dee-nee-hee.

Take me, and guide me, Jehovah,
I am walking through this barren land,
I am weak, but thou art mighty.
Help me.
Help me...to help my Rose."

When Rose awoke, the face of the woman came to her full force. She had beautiful long black hair and compassionate eyes. The song she had sung lodged in her mind, the words still on her lips as Rose struggled to stand. It was a Cherokee song. Where had she heard it before?

Then she remembered...Grandpa had sung it to her and told her it was a song that the Cherokee people had sung on the Trail of Tears.

She found that she had renewed strength and determination to continue. Wonder filled her. Who was this beautiful image who asked for help? Who was this protector who wanted to help her?

She took a deep breath, steeling herself for the pain she knew would come when she moved her foot. She picked up her stick, leaned on it and limped out of the cave. She looked up at the cloudless sky. The warm sunshine sliced through the trees, piercing the fog. Now she could see to begin her search again. And with the thought of a protector watching over her, she even smiled.

Each step was more difficult but with strong determination she moved forward, following her instinct. She was hot. Perspiration stood out on her head. She knew that she had fever, but she kept moving. With her head bent low, and pausing often to rest, she hobbled onward, breathing heavily. She was stopping more often now and at times felt as if she could not take another step. Leaning against a tree she rested. Standing still allowed her to hear a sound in the distance. It sounded like splashing water.

"Am I hallucinating?" she whispered aloud.

As she limped closer to the sound, she was sure that it sounded like moving water.

Nearer and nearer she inched her way, parting tree limbs and bushes, receiving cuts on her face and arms in her haste to get to the water. She was certain that it was the river...it had to be...yes! It had to be the river!

Moving a bushy limb out of her way she drew a quick breath.

She had found, not the river, but a waterfall where the height of it spanned the side of a mountain. For a moment she felt disappointed.

"It's not the river...but somewhere there has to be a creek that will point the way to it." Her thoughts clouded, it took a while before she could focus once again. Relief came then. "All I have to do is follow the creek."

Her gaze now took in the scene before her...the beautiful waterfall. Water...cool clear spring water! Thirst came full force then, as she listened to the welcomed sound of the water pouring over the rocks. She limped forward, gasping in pain with every step, but smiling, her eyes riveted on the scene before her.

"I will survive," she said. "Lone Wolfe, I am coming back to you!"

Reaching the waterfall's edge she waded into the pool, unaware of the icy water. Standing there in the rushing coolness, tears filled her eyes as she silently thanked her Protector.

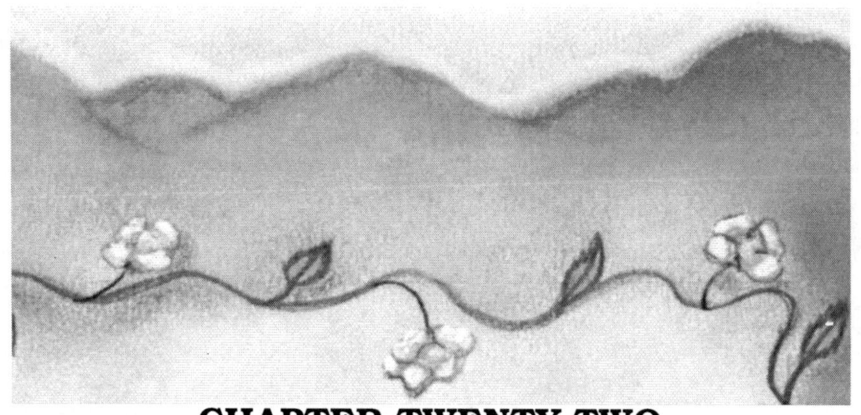

CHAPTER TWENTY-TWO
Face in the Waterfall

After Rose had satisfied her thirst she sat down on a large rock at the bottom of the waterfall. The misty spray from the water flowing down the mountain covered her body. Easing her injured foot into a small eddy of water she hoped that the coldness would relieve some of the pain.

This is a beautiful place she thought, looking around.

The forest was dotted with dogwood trees in full bloom. Their white flowers stood out among the new bright green leaves of the trees.

Rose sat looking at the high waterfall, marveling at its beauty. Her gaze was drawn to one wide stream of water cascading down the side of the waterfall. She sat staring at it. Suddenly the image of the same woman she had seen in the fog appeared. She leaned forward trying to see her clearer.

The woman smiled. She slowly raised her arm, pointed away from the waterfall and then nodded to Rose.

Rose struggled to stand to look closer at her, but when she did the woman was gone, leaving only the cascading waters shouting her message of hope.

Again Rose felt that a protector was helping her find her way back to Lone Wolfe. She would walk in the direction the woman had pointed for her to follow.

Rose stood, groaning with pain, but with renewed encouragement. She knew that she must continue to move, no matter how painful.

"I will follow the creek," Rose whispered aloud. "It goes underneath the ground. It will eventually flow into the river, and if I can find the river I can find Lone Wolfe."

Rose looked in the direction the woman had pointed and searched the area. Finally she saw where the water resurfaced into a little stream of water below the waterfall. She limped to the edge of it and saw that it widened, leading away from the waterfall.

There was no path to follow, but Rose pushed her way through the dense foliage. She didn't notice that her face and arms were bleeding—bleeding from scratches and bruises left there by bushes through which she made her way.

At one time Rose lost sight of the creek, but her determination forced her forward and once again she found the water, her leader. She had not been traveling long when she glimpsed something in the distance. She stopped and parted the leaves of a cascading rhododendron plant. She saw a small cabin nestled in a clearing in front of her.

She stood for a moment and saw no movement around the cabin. It looked deserted. Leaving the creek behind her she moved toward the building, hoping that there would be people living in it who could help her find her way back to Lone Wolfe. Nearing it, she saw no one. The old cabin sat alone, empty.

It beckoned to her and she answered its call.

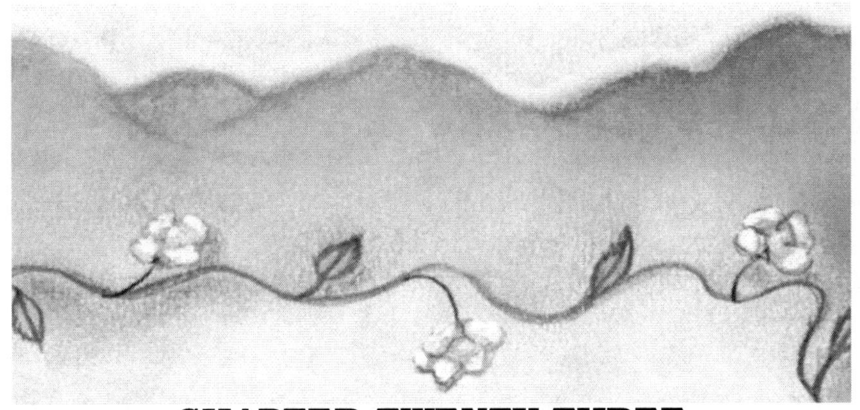

CHAPTER TWENTY-THREE

Manna From Heaven

Rose limped toward the little cabin sitting on a rise in front of the tall mountains behind it. She looked for a path leading to the cabin, but found none.

Just before she reached the house she looked down and saw large flat rocks that once served as a walkway to the cabin from the creek. While she followed them she glanced to one side of the cabin and saw large stones stacked to make a wall fence. Now half of them had fallen away and others were covered with moss and weeds. Looking to the other side of the house she noticed a large clearing of level ground. That was once a garden spot she thought. Weeds and small trees now claimed the land.

When Rose reached the cabin she stopped

before it, taking in the structure. The front porch reached across the length of the house. There was no door at the open doorway and it told her that the cabin had been abandoned for a long time.

When she started to limp up the steps she stopped suddenly. Something caught her eye at her feet. She gasped!

There at the foot of the steps lay a white feather.

Slowly Rose stooped and picked it up. A warm feeling surged through her body. She took the feather and slowly brushed it across her cheek, remembering that this was the second feather she had found. She slipped it deeply into her pocket, pushing it as low as she could, not wanting to lose this one.

Leaning on her stick she limped up the steps and peered inside. A slight breeze blew through the cabin and she could smell the dusty odor of the old building.

She saw that the cabin was divided into two rooms. She moved slowly into the first room, stepping over the door that had fallen and lay on the floor. She stood in the center of the small room and looked around. Wide wooden planks formed the floor. The walls were also wide planks of wood of irregular sizes. The chink between them had washed away with time and Rose could see the sunlight filtering into the room between the boards, adding soft light to the room.

She moved on to the adjoining room. She recognized it as being the kitchen with a few empty food cans discarded in disarray.

A cupboard stood in the corner of the room

with one door missing from its front. Rose made her way to it and slowly opened the remaining door...and caught her breath with relief and then smiled. In it, left behind by the cabin's occupants, were two jars of food...food!

She quickly picked up a jar and looked closely at it. It held tomatoes—tomatoes she could eat. She then discovered that the other jar held peaches. Dropping to her knees, she set the jars on the floor and unscrewed the lid of the tomatoes. Using the ring she popped the lid. She then opened the peaches. Dipping her fingers into each jar she brought the food to her mouth. Tomato juice ran down her fingers and around her arm mixed with the juice of the peaches. Not even noticing, she ate until the contents of both jars were gone. Manna from heaven, she thought.

She rose, leaving the jars on the floor and looked around the room more carefully. In a corner sat an old rocking chair, one arm broken off, and an old seed catalog on the floor beside it. On one wall a man's shirt hung on a wooden peg. Rose quickly removed her still damp clothes and slipped it on over her tired body. It covered her almost to her knees and she felt warmer.

Looking over at the fireplace on the other side of the room she wished that it held a roaring fire so that she could warm herself.

The fireplace had been built of rocks collected from the creek and was now blackened from the many fires built in it throughout the years. The mantel above it was one half of a log and Rose noticed that there was something on top of it. She walked over to the mantel, reached up and found a large box of Diamond matches. To her surprise the saved matches were dry. She took one match out and closed the box. Striking it she held her breath. The flame leaped and Rose smiled.

I will build a fire, dry my clothes and warm

myself, then move on, she thought, reaching for her stick. She limped outside and collected twigs and small limbs and returned to build a fire.

Lying on the floor in the warmth of the flames with a full stomach the thankful woman went to sleep.

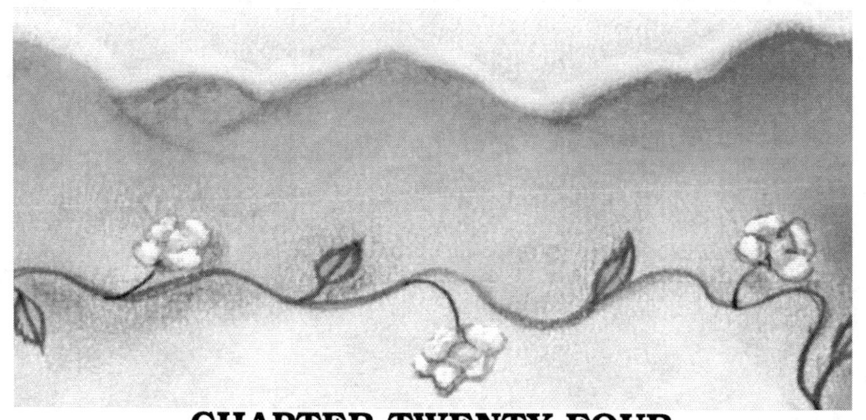

CHAPTER TWENTY-FOUR

The Rock-Face Mountain

Rose awoke suddenly. The fire had gone out and for a moment she did not recognize her surroundings. She sat up and stretched. Her body ached and was sore from lying on the hard wooden floor, but she knew that she could not stay in the little cabin. She reached for her stick and pulled herself to her feet. Finding her clothes dry, she put them on. Leaning on the stick, she limped out of the cabin and on toward the creek.

Each step was more difficult but with strong determination she moved forward. She was hot, perspiration stood out on her head in large beads. She knew that she had fever, but she kept moving. With her head bent low, and stopping often to rest, she hobbled onward, breathing heavily.

She was pausing more often now and at times she felt that she could not take another step. The two jars of food had given her a little strength but now the days of pain and hunger were closing in on her. Leaning on a tree she stopped, almost surrendering to the blackness threatening to engulf her.

"I will not give up now. I will survive," she whispered. "I will see Lone Wolfe again."

She straightened her body and limped forward. Again she stopped. Sitting down to rest, she realized that she had not been following the creek. She could see it no longer. She closed her eyes and lay down on the ground. She felt that she could not take another step.

Suddenly she opened her eyes. Lying there on the ground, she could hear the strength of movement within the earth. The power of water underneath the mountainside tingled her face.

"Am I feeling things?" she whispered aloud.

She pulled herself up, listening intently. There it was—the river. She knew it was the river! She rose, and almost ran through foliage, to burst out onto the riverbank!

Rose heaved a sigh of relief, smiled and then laughed out loud. Tears followed mixed with great gulps of air.

"Finally! I found it!" she cried and listened for a moment to the welcomed sound of the water rushing over the rocks. Now, limping forward, gasping in pain with every step, she pushed herself even closer, her eyes riveted on the river.

Reaching the edge she waded in, again splashing water onto her face, unaware of the icy water, and cried out. "Thank you! Thank you!"

The grateful woman waded deeper into the rushing water, its healing powers whipping across her legs. The river water was cold, but thirst took command over the shock she felt in its icy clutches. Rose cupped her hand, leaned over and filled it, drinking deeply, over and over.

After she had quenched her thirst she put both hands in the river and again splashed water over her face. Limping to a large rock, she sat down on it, letting the cold water wash over her swollen foot, hoping that it would reduce some of the swelling.

Resting, she thought about Lone Wolfe. More tears formed in Rose's eyes remembering the cruel way Clem had treated him. She was certain that he was seriously injured, but she refused to believe that he was dead...but then, she thought, he could be...NO! I will not believe that!

Her thoughts raced on. Who was the man who had been so cruel? Where did he come from? She supposed that she would never know. Well, she thought again, he will not hurt anyone now. The man is dead.

Rose began to feel stronger and soon stood with determination.

Which way do I go, she suddenly asked herself. How do I find my direction? She looked around, allowing her gaze to travel over the horizon. There's the rock-faced mountain Lone Wolfe showed me from his front porch! I see it above me. Her thoughts grew wild. It can't be far...I can find my way!

Hours later as she came within sight of the cabin. she began to call out Lone Wolfe's name again and again. Soon she had hobbled to the cabin and had slowly made her way up the steps, clinging to the rail to keep from falling. She flung the door open and limped inside. When her eyes adjusted to the dimly lit room, she screamed.

There was a large blood stain on the floor. She limped from room to room shouting Lone Wolfe's name, frightened when she could not find him.

"Where is he?"

She looked wildly around the room, then went back into the bedroom.

"A bear" she thought in terror. "NO! NO!"

Crying, sobbing loudly, she collapsed on the bed and lost consciousness.

Later that day the forest rangers found Rose in the cabin when they returned from searching the woods for her.

They summoned an ambulance, and then while waiting, the lawmen shook their heads in disbelief. They wondered where Rose had been for the past three days.

"Some strong woman, huh," said one forest ranger to another.

"Had to be...to get away from that escaped convict!" responded the second man. "Wonder what happened?'

"And where is he?" asked the other forest ranger as his glance swept across the mountains.

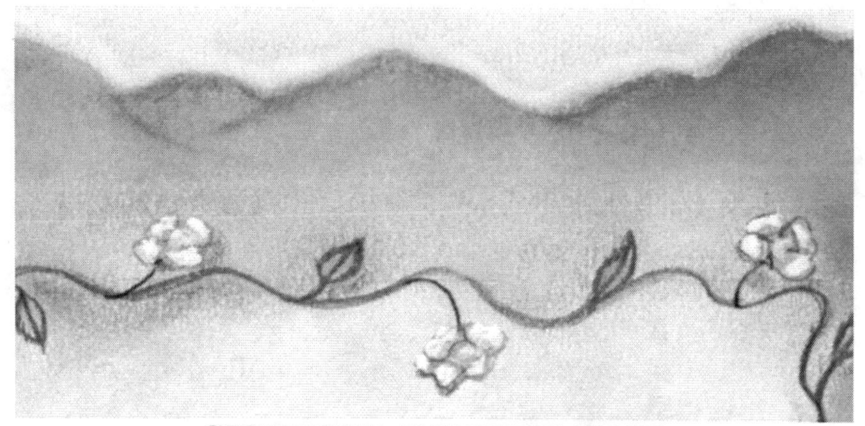

CHAPTER TWENTY-FIVE
Meanwhile—the Friday Before

Friday night Anna and Grandpa had been listening to the news on the radio while they ate supper.

"We interrupt this program to bring you a special bulletin...local law enforcement officers are searching for a prisoner who escaped from a roadside work detail late yesterday afternoon. He is believed to be hiding in the Smoky Mountains area of Chilohee. If he is spotted do not approach him as he is considered dangerous. If you have information concerning this man call the local sheriff's office at 924-5903 or police station, 482-2693."

"Grandpa, did you hear that?" Anna asked, pausing from eating, her fork in midair.

"Yes." The old man nodded.

"Lone Wolfe is up there and his cabin is in that area. He could be in danger."

She rose from the table and walked hurriedly toward the living room to the telephone. "I'm going to call the sheriff's office," she added over her shoulder.

"Rose is up there too," Grandpa said.

"What?" Anna stopped and turned back to look at Grandpa.

"Went today."

Anna whirled around and ran to the telephone, fear clouding her vision.

When she returned to the table she sat down and patted Grandpa's shoulder. "The sheriff said that he would send a group of lawmen up to the cabin to investigate the first thing in the morning."

"Good."

"I wish we could call Lone Wolfe," Anna said. "I worry when he's up there where he can't be reached. And now Rose is at the cabin."

Grandpa nodded.

Early the next morning the lawmen arrived and saw only one vehicle outside the cabin but no sign of life or movement.

"Maybe they left," one of the men said.

The other nodded. "I hope so."

They knocked on the cabin door and when they received no response they entered and found Lone Wolfe unconscious on the floor. His head lay in a puddle of blood seeping from his head wounds."

"Is he alive?" the deputy asked his partner who was stooping down to examine Lone Wolfe.

"Yes, but barely breathing. He's lost a lot of blood. I'm not sure he's going to make it...call an ambulance...quick."

The deputy untied Lone Wolfe while the other called for immediate help.

Realizing that time was critical for Lone Wolfe's survival they did not wait for the ambulance to arrive. Instead they laid Lone Wolfe on the back seat of the patrol car and started down the mountain. When they met the ambulance on the road Lone Wolfe was moved to the emergency vehicle and transported to the hospital.

"Did you find the girl?' the ambulance driver asked.

"No. Her van is gone. She may have come down the mountain to get help, but we're going back up the mountain to search for her anyway."

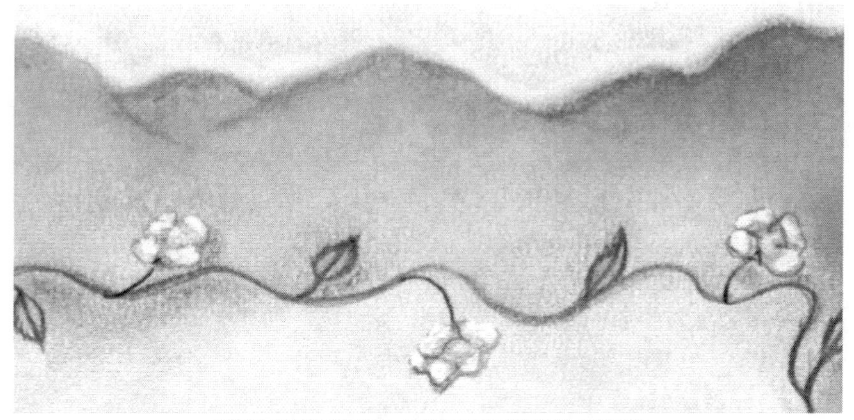

CHAPTER TWENTY-SIX

A Telling of a Tale

When Rose opened her eyes she looked around and realized that she was lying in a hospital room. She tried to get out of bed, but the tubes attached to the machine by the bed restricted her movement. Raising her head she could see that her foot was in a heavy cast.

Lone Wolfe, she thought, tears springing to her eyes. Where is he?

She heard a soft knock and she looked toward the door as it slowly opened.

A familiar face smiled at Rose. "Good morning, sleepy head. I went out to get some coffee. I'm glad you are finally awake," Tara smiled and walked to her friend's bedside.

"Lone Wolfe...where is....?" Rose raised her head and attempted to sit up.

"Sh-h-h. Don't try to get up. You are too weak," said Tara, gently pushing Rose back down on the bed.

"Lone Wolfe...where is he? Is he going to be all right?"

"Yes," Tara smiled. "He's going to be fine...in time. He has had some very severe head wounds, but he will recover."

"Are you sure?"

"Yes!" smiled Tara. "He has a hard head...look how long it took him to ask you out."

"Where is he?"

"Right here in this hospital. I'm sure that he will be in to see you as soon as he regains some of his strength."

"I'm going to see him. I...." Rose tried to get out of bed again, but fell back on the pillow, exhausted.

"Be patient. He's not going anywhere. You can see him later," Tara said, patting Rose on the shoulder. "He's sleeping a lot."

"When did you come?"

"Yesterday, as soon as I heard about you and Lone Wolfe. You two gave me quite a scare."

Rose managed a slight smile.

"I spent the night with you."

"You did?"

"Yes."

"Thank you. Lone Wolfe? Who is with him?"

"His mother...and Dovie, when she's not in school."

A knock on the door interrupted the young women's conversation and both of them glanced toward the door.

The local sheriff opened the door slightly

and looked in the room. He cleared his throat.

"May I come in?" he said.

"Yes," answered Rose.

"How are you feeling, Rose?"

"Better now that I am home."

The sheriff smiled at Rose, hesitated momentarily, then said slowly, "Rose, do you feel up to telling me what happened to you and Lone Wolfe at the cabin?"

"Yes."

"The man who abducted you is an escaped convict. Did you know that?"

Rose shook her head.

"Do you know anything about him? We haven't found him yet."

Rose frowned, suddenly remembering the cries in the woods.

"You don't have to talk now, Rose, if you don't feel like it," Tara leaned over and whispered to Rose when she saw the frown on her friend's face.

"It's all right. I will tell you." She paused, and then began speaking softly. "It was a terrible time for Lone Wolfe and me," and then she began relating the incidents that occurred on the mountain. She stopped occasionally to wipe tears away from her eyes when she told about the physical abuse Lone Wolfe had received from the convict. She paused briefly, then continued describing her abduction and concluded by telling about the bear attack. "You can halt your search for him. He is dead."

There was complete silence in the room after Rose finished.

The sheriff had listened intently to every

detail Rose had described, shaking his head often in sorrow for the experiences the two young people had endured.

"You are a strong young woman, Rose," he said, "and courageous too."

"It's over. I'm so thankful that Lone Wolfe and I are alive."

"Yes." The sheriff reached over and took Rose's hand. "Thank you for talking to me. I will be back to see you again."

"Thank you," Rose replied and then drifted off into a much-needed peaceful sleep.

Tara smiled at Rose, then leaned down and gently pushed a strand of hair away from her face. "I will be back, my friend," she whispered, then tiptoed quietly out of the room.

As the door closed behind them, a swaying of the gauzy curtains framed a beautiful butterfly fluttering at the window...a good omen of new life to come.

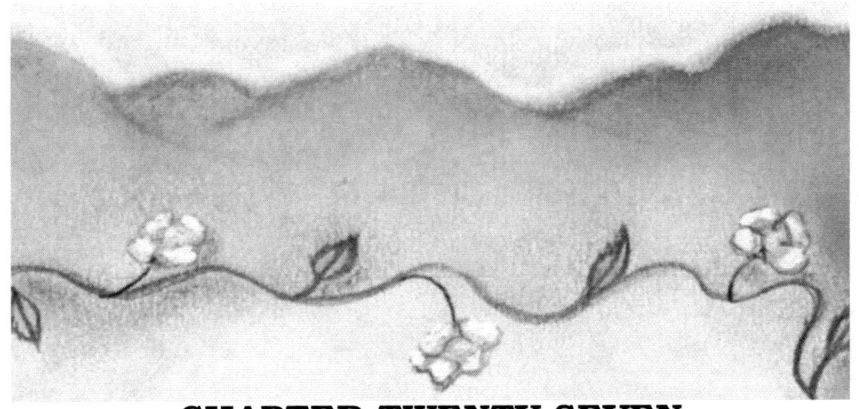

CHAPTER TWENTY-SEVEN

A Year Later

Spring had arrived early, returning with its burst of bright green leaves on the trees and many colorful flowers.

The event of the previous year was seldom mentioned by Rose or Lone Wolfe. It was an experience both of them wanted to forget. They had recuperated quickly from the physical wounds and the experience deepened their love for each other.

Rose had not talked much about her days lost in the woods...except with Grandpa. Somehow she knew he would understand the unusual things that happened to her in the woods. When she told him about the woman, her protector, he nodded, but said nothing. He had listened carefully when she described the cabin...and then he said, "I know about the cabin you found."

"You do?"

"Yes."

"Have you ever seen it before, Grandpa?"

He smiled. "Yes, it is where I lived until I came here to live with Anna."

"Grandpa!" Rose said, surprised, "You lived there?"

"Yes... for many, many years. My wife and I raised all of our children in that little cabin. Lone Wolfe's Mother was born in the very room where you found the food jars."

"And Grandpa! That was your shirt I found!"

"Yes," he nodded.

"Did you build the little fireplace?"

Again he nodded.

"Thanks for leaving the matches," she laughed.

He joined her laughter.

"Grandpa, how did you get to town from way out there in the woods?"

"I walked."

"Walked? That's a long walk."

"Only way I had to travel. We had no car...and there were no roads."

"Oh, I know about that!" Rose smiled.

"I carried food that I grew in a garden behind the cabin and traded it in town for things we needed."

Grandpa told Rose how he once killed a bear in the front yard of the house.

"Is the bear claw you wear from the bear you killed?

"Yes," Grandpa laughed. "I was a very young man then."

Rose sat and watched Grandpa as he talked on and on, enjoying all his stories as he related many things that occurred in the little cabin where she had found refuge.

Later, Lone Wolfe and Rose sat in the porch swing enjoying the warm spring afternoon.

"Rose," Lone Wolfe said softly, looking into her eyes. "Do you think that you will ever want to visit my cabin again?"

"Of course," she answered quickly, smiling at Lone Wolfe.

"Really?" he ask, surprised at her immediate response.

"Yes. I love the cabin and the beautiful scenery around it."

"I didn't think you would want to go back after what happened last spring."

"But I do. We have made happy memories there," she smiled. "We will try to forget the bad one we experienced." Leaning her head on his shoulder, she continued, "Now we can make new good memories."

Lone Wolfe smiled at Rose thinking that she continued to amaze him.

"I am so glad you feel that way." He gathered her into his arms and kissed her. "I was afraid that you might never want to go back to the cabin again." He paused, then ventured. "Would you like to go any time soon?"

"Yes...and very soon," she answered.

"Good. How about next weekend?" anticipation sounding in his voice.

"Yes. That would be nice."

Lone Wolfe smiled to himself thinking about his long awaited surprise.

"I will go up Thursday morning and you can come up when you get out of school on Friday."

"Fine."

"There's just one thing...before you go to the cabin Grandpa wants you to come by to see him. He has something to tell you."

"He does?"

"Yes."

An amused grin played across Lone Wolfe's face.

"What is it?"

"Can't tell you," Lone Wolfe laughed. "He'd have my hide."

"Please," Rose begged, hugging Lone Wolfe close to her.

"Nope!" Lone Wolfe grinned, thinking about the plans for the coming week-end. "You'll see."

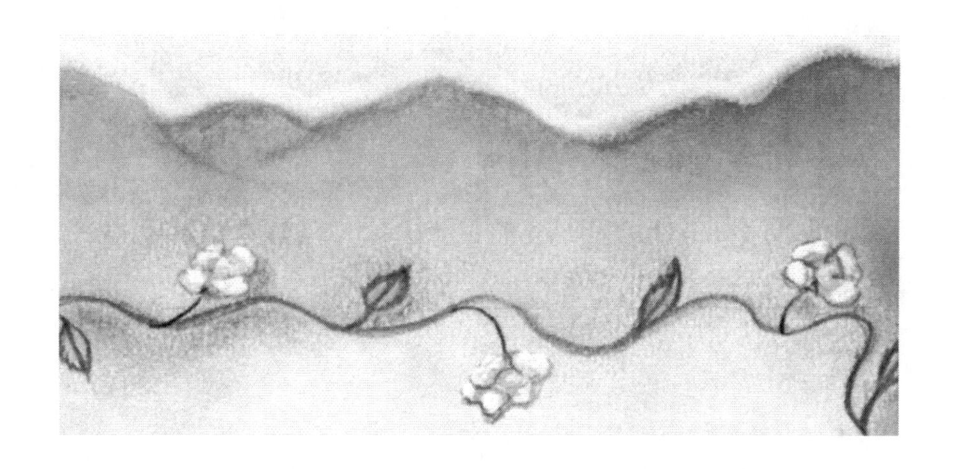

CHAPTER TWENTY-EIGHT
Heritage Unfolds

Rose was anxious to get to Lone Wolfe's cabin. She left school and hurriedly went to see Grandpa, wondering what could be so urgent that he would want her to delay her trip by stopping by to see him on the way.

But she loved spending time with the old man. He told her about his youthful years and his adventures, and Rose drank in every word, forgetting none of his stories. She had great respect for the Cherokee elder and his great wisdom.

"Rose, I want to tell you something today," he began as soon as she arrived.

"Yes, Grandpa?" she said, sitting down and pulling her chair close to him, not wanting to miss a word.

"You go to the Georgia cemetery often, don't you?"

"Yes, I do, Grandpa."

He nodded, then looked at her.

Rose waited patiently for him to continue.

"I want to tell you something, Rose...tell it to you myself...that is why I asked you to come here today." He paused, looking into Rose's eyes. "I wanted to be sure that what I tell you is correct, that is why I've had to wait until now."

What is he going to tell me? thought Rose, clearly puzzled by his words.

"Lone Wolfe has been doing research for me."

Research? thought Rose. Why?

"Rose...."

"Yes?" Rose leaned toward Grandpa.

"I know...." he said quietly. "I know about your parents."

Surprise showed on Rose's face. "My parents?"

"Yes. I know who they were."

Rose was stunned and said nothing for a moment, then got out of the chair and knelt on the floor beside Grandpa.

"Lone Wolfe has been searching ancestral rolls for almost a year. We have talked about what he has found." Grandpa took Rose's hand and looked directly into her eyes. "Rose?"

"Yes." she whispered, moving closer. She swallowed hard and stared into Grandpa's face.

"Rose, your father was a white man, but

your mother was a Cherokee woman."

"What?" Rose's hand covered her mouth. "What do you mean, Grandpa?"

"She was an Indian, Rose...a Cherokee."

"Why didn't my family tell me?"

Grandpa shook his head slowly from side to side.

"Where are my parents buried?"

"In Oklahoma."

Rose looked down and clasped her hands tightly.

"White Feather was...." Grandpa began softly.

"White Feather?" Rose interrupted.

Grandpa leaned over and took Rose's hand. "You are a descendant of White Feather, Rose."

"What?"

Grandpa smiled and nodded. "Yes...a great, great, great Granddaughter."

Rose stood and then sat back down in her chair, not speaking. She sat there in the overwhelming silence of the room, trying to understand all she had heard.

Grandpa became silent for a moment and then asked, "Do you know about the Cherokee Clans, Rose?"

"I know that there are seven."

"Yes. Our family is of the Long Hair Clan. White Feather was of the Paint Clan. Now your clan is Paint also." The elder sat quietly, looking at Rose, waiting for her to speak.

She looked questioningly at Grandpa and said, "The other people in the cemetery...who are they, Grandpa?"

"Your relatives...well, most of them. The

others were friends...and our relatives, Rose. We are descendants of Tsu-la. After his white wife Marie died, Tsu-la married a Cherokee woman. Our family descended from them."

"Did you know any of White Feather's people, Grandpa?"

"Oh, yes. They told me many stories about White Feather. You are much like her, Rose...the same courage, determination and strength. You proved that last spring when you were lost in the mountains."

Rose sat quietly thinking about White Feather and her grave...remembering how she was drawn to it each time she visited the cemetery.

"I did not want to tell you until I had all of the facts and it has taken Lone Wolfe and me a long time to find out about your ancestors. I knew when I first met you...when you came for Christmas dinner...that you were a Cherokee woman. Remember I asked you about it?"

"Yes."

"There were other signs too," he smiled at Rose.

"What signs, Grandpa?"

"The sound of the Cherokee drums touched your heart, and the day you found the white feather at White Feather's grave." He took Rose's hand and smiled. "Rose, you are Cherokee."

"Grandpa, that makes me very happy," she said, rising quickly and throwing her arms around his neck, hugging him tightly. Happy tears flowed down her face. "Thank you, thank you for finding out all of this for me. Gv-ge-yu (I love you), Grandpa."

Grandpa nodded and patted Rose on the

back. "I found out all of this to be true only a few days ago and I could not wait any longer to tell you."

Rose stood and smiled at Grandpa through misty eyes. "Now I must go tell Lone Wolfe," she said.

"He knows, Rose," the old man chuckled.

"Of course," she laughed. "I forgot!"

Rose started toward the door.

"Wait!"

Rose turned around. "Yes, Grandpa?"

"There is something else."

Respectfully Rose walked back to the Cherokee elder.

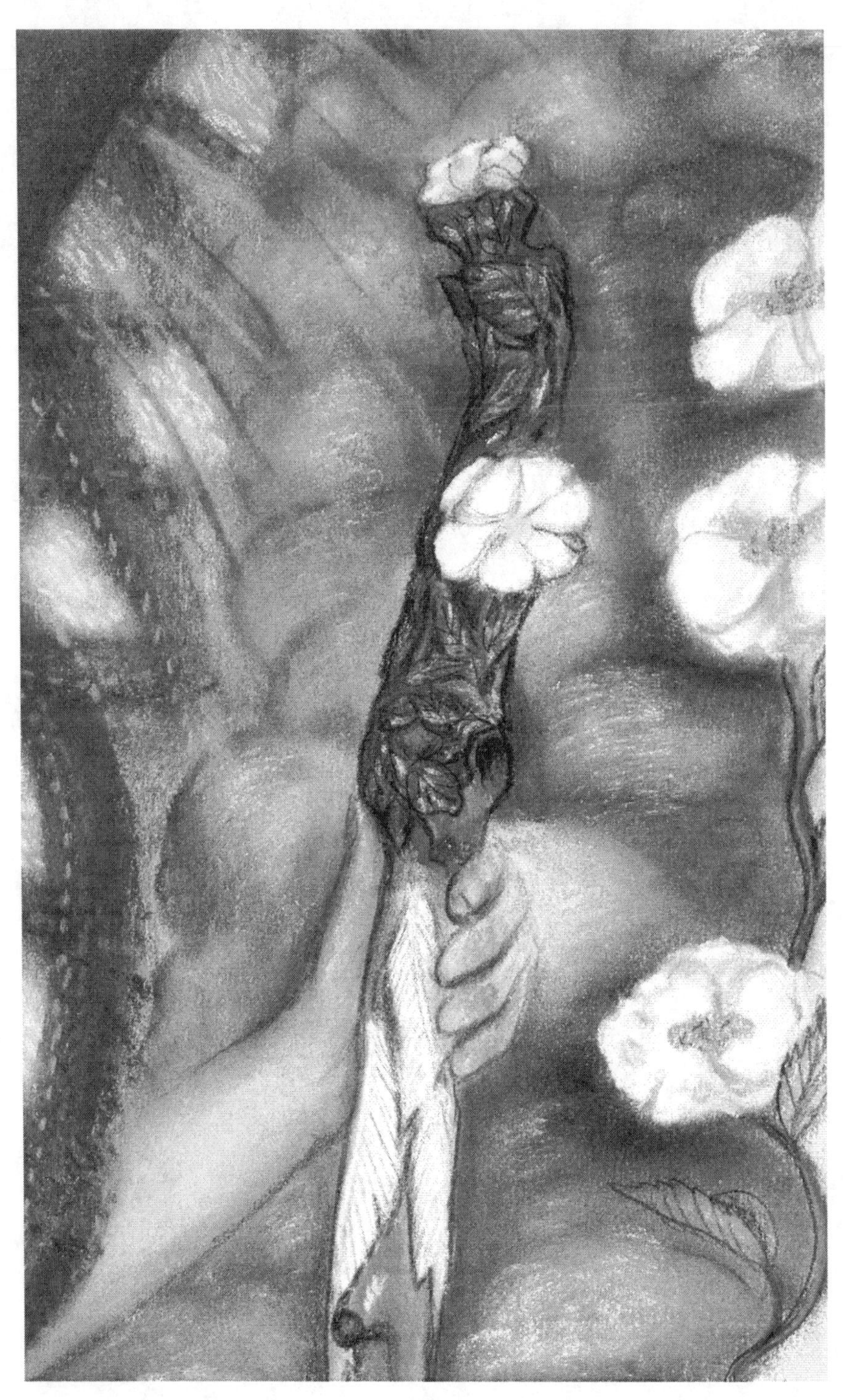

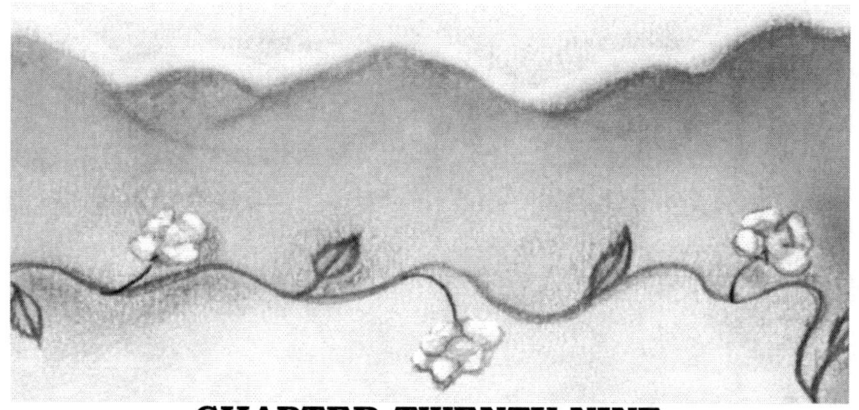

CHAPTER TWENTY-NINE

The Gift

Grandpa rolled his wheelchair to a nearby closet and reached inside. He brought out a tall hiking stick.

"Look at this, Rose," he said, rolling his chair back to face her. He handed the staff to her.

"It's beautiful, Grandpa," she said, stroking the carvings on the stick.

"I have been saving it for you until I could tell you about your ancestors."

"The wood is very pretty and it's hand carved, isn't it?" Rose asked, fingering the roses and feathers carved and painted near the top of the stick.

Grandpa nodded. "It is made of the wood of the dogwood tree. You have heard of the Cherokee Little People, haven't you?"

"Yes."

"Well, the Dogwood Clan of the Little People lives among the dogwood trees. They look for beauty in everyone and in all things. They look for the good in people. They respect Mother Nature. They care for everything that Mother Nature provides and they like the people that do that...like you, Rose."

Rose turned the stick over and over in her hands and gently ran her hand up and down its shaft.

"It's so beautiful. It's very old, isn't it?"

"Yes...many, many years old."

"Did you carve it, Grandpa?"

"No. Long ago Tsu-la carved this stick."

Rose looked quickly at Grandpa, her eyes widening. "The Tsu-la who is buried in the Georgia cemetery?" she said, remembering his grave.

Grandpa nodded. "Yes. He gave it to White Feather. After she died her daughter Little Fawn gave it to Tsu-la's granddaughter, and later she gave it to me. I have owned it since I was a very young boy."

Rose sat down on the floor and kept turning the stick over in her hands, stroking each delicate pattern of the roses and feathers carved and painted on it.

Grandpa watched Rose, smiling. "The name of the rose on the stick is the Cherokee Rose. It's the flower you found growing beside White Feather's grave."

"I remember."

"Rose," Grandpa said, leaning closer, "I want you to have this stick now. I know that you will always cherish it."

"Oh, Grandpa, I couldn't accept this. It is your family's treasured heirloom."

"But now it will go back to White Feather's family again," he smiled. "You must take it. You are White Feather's descendant."

Tears of joy slid down Rose's face. She rose and went into Grandpa's arms, hugging him. "Ski (thank you)," she said, using a Cherokee word, pleasing Grandpa. "I will always treasure and take care of it."

"Now go. Lone Wolfe is waiting for you... Cherokee Rose." And the old man smiled.

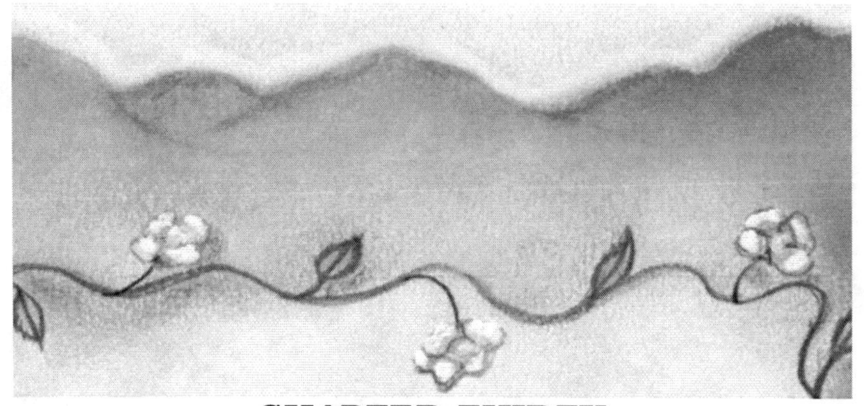

CHAPTER THIRTY

The Spirit of White Feather

Rose hummed softly while she drove to Lone Wolfe's cabin. Several times she lovingly stroked the hiking stick which lay on the seat beside her.

What a wonderful treasure Grandpa has given me today, she thought, glancing at the stick. She smiled thinking about how much she loved the Cherokee elder.

She was filled with awe at learning about her parents and had so many unanswered questions concerning them. But finally she knew something about her heritage. She wondered where her parents were buried in Oklahoma. She would like to visit their graves. She would find out more about them on her next visit to see Grandpa.

The sun was beginning to disappear behind the mountains when Rose arrived at the cabin. She parked her van in front of the cabin and smiled. Looking up at the tall stone chimney she saw wispy smoke rising from it. Lone Wolfe had built a fire for her.

She got out of the van with the hiking stick in her hand and hurried up the steps and tried to open the door. She turned the knob several times and then realized that it was locked.

That's strange, she thought, I know that Lone Wolfe is inside. I hear music playing and his truck is here. She tried to open the door again.

"Lone Wolfe! Lone Wolfe!" she called, knocking on the door, beginning to panic.

"Rose, I'll be right there," he answered from within the cabin.

"What's going on?" Rose whispered. She thought that it was very odd that Lone Wolfe had locked the door knowing that she was coming.

Slowly the door opened to the cabin. Lone Wolfe stepped out on the deck and hugged Rose, and then moved back.

Before he could speak Rose held the staff in front of him.

"Look, Lone Wolfe! Look what Grandpa gave me!"

"Yes," he smiled. "We thought that you would be pleased to have it."

"Oh yes!" Rose said. "I love it! It's so beautiful!"

"And so are you, Rose," he said, looking into her eyes, then taking the stick from her he stepped aside. "Come inside, Rose."

Rose walked through the doorway, and slowly entered the dimly lit room.

She gasped!

The cabin was bathed in the golden glow of candles, their strength flickering all over the room. Rose turned in a circle. Candles were everywhere.

Lone Wolfe stood to the side and watched Rose. He wanted to remember everything about her on this special evening. He wanted to record every little detail in his mind. She was wearing a dress he had never seen before of soft material that clung to her body, accenting her narrow waist. The dress was light pink and she wore a silver chain around her neck centered with a small turquoise stone. Her earrings were loops made of silver and turquoise.

Rose clasped her hands in front of her and looked at Lone Wolfe.

"It's beautiful," she whispered.

Lone Wolfe smiled, looking at her dark hair hanging loosely around her shoulders. He loved the way it bounced when she moved.

Rose turned and looked around the room again. A small table in the middle of the room was set for dinner and in the center of it sat a birthday cake.

"Oh, Lone Wolfe! How did you know it is my birthday?"

"Grandpa told me," he laughed. "He knows everything."

"Yes," she smiled. "Yes, he does. This is wonderful! Thank you!"

"I'm glad you like it."

"Like it? I love it!"

She ran to Lone Wolfe and hugged him.

Stepping back from him she said, "Lone Wolfe, I truly appreciate all the work you did for me. I am so proud to be a Cherokee. You and Grandpa are the only ones who ever cared enough about me to help me know who I really am."

Lone Wolfe smiled.

"Before we eat there is something outside I want to show you before it gets too dark. Come," Lone Wolfe said, taking Rose by the arm and guiding her to the deck and down the steps. Taking her hand he led to the corner of the front yard and pointed to a plant.

"I planted this today in your honor."

"Me?"

"Yes," he said, putting his arm around her. "This is a Cherokee Rose bush."

"That's the same kind of plant that grows by White Feather's grave," Rose said thoughtfully, leaning over and fingering the leaves on the bush. "Grandpa told me one of the legends about it."

"Soon it will have beautiful blooms on it," Lone Wolfe smiled.

"Thank you, Lone Wolfe," Rose said, hugging him.

"You are welcome," he said, kissing her lightly and then leading her back into the cabin.

"Are you hungry?"

"Yes."

"Sit down and I will bring the food," he said, helping Rose into a chair.

Watching Lone Wolfe put the meal before her Rose asked in amazement, "Where did all this food come from? Did you cook it?"

"No," he laughed, "I brought it up from home. I had help...busybodies full of love."

After they had eaten Lone Wolfe lit the candles on the birthday cake. “Make a wish,” he said.

Looking at the flickering candles for a moment Rose closed her eyes, then opened them, leaned over and blew out the candles.

“Did you make a good wish?” teased Lone Wolfe.

“Oh, yes!” Rose laughed.

When they finished eating Lone Wolfe suggested that they go outside and sit on the deck for a while.

“There’s a full moon tonight,” Lone Wolfe said.

They walked outside with their arms around each other and stood by the deck railing, looking at the night sky sprinkled with stars.

“The moon is rising,” Lone Wolfe said, nodding toward the mountains in front of them.

“Yes, it’s beautiful.”

“Rose, I...” Lone Wolfe stammered.

“Lone Wolfe, are you all right?” Rose asked, turning to look at him.

“Yes. Why do you ask?”

“You seem a little nervous tonight.”

He did not respond. Instead he pulled Rose closer into his arms and they stood looking at the moon, now hanging just above the mountain ridge in front of them. Katydids filled the night with their loud singing.

“It’s so beautiful here,” sighed Rose, putting her head on Lone Wolfe’s shoulder.

“Let’s sit down, Rose,” Lone Wolfe whispered softly, motioning to the porch swing. “There is something I really need to say and I can’t keep it inside me any longer.”

"All right."

They sat quietly for a moment before Lone Wolfe turned to Rose and took her hand.

"Rose, look at me," he said seriously.

Rose shifted her body and gazed into Lone Wolfe's face.

"Rose?"

"Yes?"

"I love you."

"I love you, too."

"Will you marry me?"

Warm happiness spread throughout her body with such force, she trembled. Rose jumped up and with strength she never realized she had, pulled Lone Wolfe to his feet.

"Oh, Lone Wolfe," she whispered, "I have a past and now I have a future!"

And in the shadow of the full moon Lone Wolfe kissed Rose, then whispered, "Gv-ge-yu, my Cherokee Rose, I love you."

"And that is the story I have wanted to tell you for so long, Janie," Rose said, reaching over to her Granddaughter and patting her hand.

"Oh, Grandmother, that was so beautiful," the young woman said with a tremor in her voice. "It was all about you, wasn't it?"

Rose smiled and nodded slowly, looking at Janie through misty eyes.

"White Feather is your grandmother too," Rose said, brushing a small tear away from her cheek.

"And this is where she lived," said Janie looking all around.

"Yes, right here on this rise facing the river."

Both sat quietly for a moment.

"So now you know why I brought you here today. I want you to know and be proud of your family heritage," said Rose.

Janie looked at her Grandmother and nodded.

"Come, we must go. It's getting late," Rose said, taking Janie's hand.

They stood, looked down at White Feather's grave for a moment, and then the pair walked hand in hand down the hill.

When they reached the bottom, Rose paused and looked up at the mountains around them. A gentle breeze crossed her face. Rose could feel White Feather's spirit touching her and then moving on to Janie—she could see it in her Granddaughter's face.

"Grandmother, stop!"

"What is it?"

"White Feather's spirit is here. I can feel it...," Janie whispered, then smiled, "...like wings around me."

"Yes," smiled Rose, looking up and pointing to the mountains. "She is here. Her spirit will always be here among these tranquil hills and valleys of the home she loved so much. She will always be here."

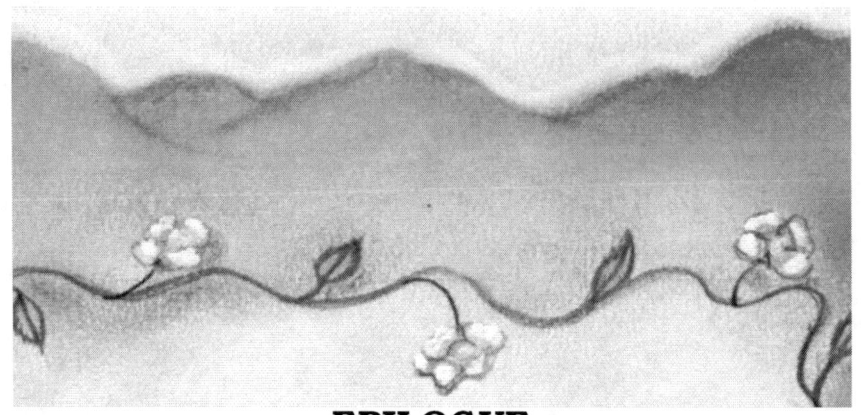

EPILOGUE

Rose opened her eyes when the flight attendant gently touched her arm to alert her that the plane had reached its destination. She had been dozing, but was now wide awake, smiling at the attendant.

She was filled with happiness from the anticipation of the upcoming event she had been eagerly awaiting. Her grandchild, Janie, was getting married in two days and Rose had come to Kentucky for the ceremony. It would be good to see her daughter, Ruth, and her three grandchildren again.

As Rose waited to leave the plane she thought about Janie. Janie had become a beautiful young woman...with gleaming black hair and dark eyes. She had recently graduated from college and very much in love with Russ, the young man who would soon become her husband.

Rose smiled as she remembered the telephone call from Janie on the night she had become engaged to her college sweetheart. She lovingly stroked the hiking stick leaning on the seat next to her. It was Janie's wedding gift...a special gift she hoped would be passed on through generations to come. Rose hoped Janie would cherish it as she herself had done during the years she had owned it.

Emily, Janie's younger sister, would soon graduate from high school, and Hunter, the youngest and only grandson, reminded her so much of Lone Wolfe. Rose swallowed, as his memory wet her eyes. Lone Wolfe...oh, how much she missed his arms around her. Shaking her head, she thought about his empty chair at home...and his desk...still cluttered.

Hunter...yes, Hunter looked like his grandfather. Even at his young age he had shown exceptional talent in artwork, enjoying drawing and painting pictures. Rose smiled through her tears. Ruth had named her son after her dad.

Now Rose was anxious to arrive and join in the wedding festivities.

Little did Rose know or realize what an important part her past influence and her strength would be needed in the future.

Janie was waiting at the gate when the plane landed. Rose hurried down the steps and rushed into Janie's arms. She felt a strange feeling pass over her...almost like the wings of a spirit had brushed her cheek. For a moment Rose remembered having this feeling many years ago when she told Janie the story of White Feather while they were in the little Georgia cemetery. Rose knew immediately that the spirit of White Feather was with her. She felt the power of love around her. Would she need White Feather's strength again or would this strength be passed on to her granddaughter for the future?

Will the power continue with Janie?

BOOKS BY NANCY
***WHITE FEATHER**
***CHEROKEE ROSE**
***JANIE OF CHEROKEE**
(A TRILOGY)
AND
***OSCAR, THE LEGENDARY ALLLIGATOR**
BOOKS CAN BE ORDERED FROM THE AUTHOR

Nancy M. Pafford
P.O. Box 528
Lakeland, GA 31635

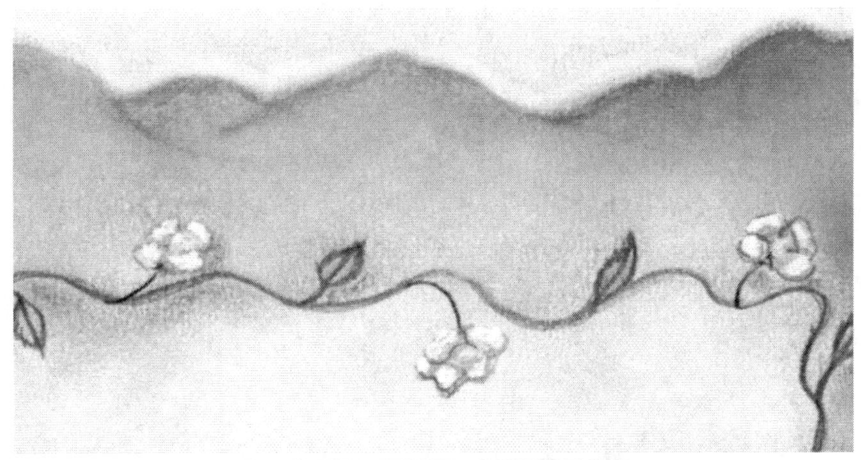

ABOUT THE AUTHOR

Nancy McIntosh Pafford resides in the Great Smoky Mountains of Cherokee, North Carolina among her Cherokee friends. She was born and reared in Waycross, Georgia, where she lived until her college days.

Nancy graduated from Georgia Teachers College (now Georgia Southern University) and moved to Lakeland, Georgia, when she married her college sweetheart, William "Fuzz" Pafford, a high school teacher and basketball coach. She taught elementary school there until she retired. She had two sons, Bryan and Tim. Tim lives in South Georgia.

After the deaths of her husband and younger son, Bryan, Nancy moved to Cheroke where she has worked for the Cherokee Historical Association promoting the drama, Unto These

Hills, and the Oconaluftee Living Indian Village. She is an associate member of the Museum of the Cherokee Indian and serves as pianist for the Cherokee United Methodist Church.

Nancy's love for the mountains and Cherokee began as a young child when she traveled there with her parents on summer vacations. Through the years she often thought that she would like to live in Cherokee and teach Cherokee children. Her dream came true, and since moving to the mountains Nancy has taught part time in the Cherokee school and says that it has been a wonderful "learning" experience.

Her love for the Cherokee culture has deepened into her very soul. This love and understanding of her adopted culture is reflected in her first book, **WHITE FEATHER**, a historical novel relating the life of a Cherokee family before, during and after the Trail of Tears. It was released in 2004 and is now in its third printing.

Nancy is working on several children's books and a collection of stories from her teaching experiences. Her avid readers are already asking for another book.